D1142457

THE HOUSE

WITH THE

LILAC SHUTTERS

Gabrielle Barnby

TP

ThunderPoint Publishing Ltd.

First Published in Great Britain in 2015 by
ThunderPoint Publishing Limited
Summit House
4-5 Mitchell Street
Edinburgh
Scotland EH6 7BD

ISBN: 978-0-9929768-8-0 (Paperback)
ISBN: 978-1-910946-02-2 (eBook)
First published 2015

www.thunderpoint.scot

Acknowledgements

I'm grateful to everyone who has helped in the production of this book particularly Seonaid and Huw Francis. Early drafts of a number of these stories received helpful comments from Sylvia Hays, Bill Ferguson, Margaret Storr, Loraine Littlejohn, Fiona Fleming and Joanna Buick. Thank you to the Stromness Writing Group for their continued criticism, support and fellowship, and especially Lucy Alsop for being such a generous reader and friend.

Thank you to my parents for a house full of books and for taking me places, to my parents-in-law for their constant support and to my husband and children for all their patience.

Dedication

For Tim

Contents

The House with the Lilac Shutters

It all started with a quick and easy method of lining a food waste bin with newspaper. I posted my suggestion to william@makedoandmend and was featured on the website as 'Tip of the day.' After that William and I became e-mail correspondents. He encouraged me to answer other queries posted on the website.

I agreed to meet him at a home-composting event at Guildford Civic Hall where he was manning a promotional stall. He was youthful looking, although I quickly realised that jet-black was not his natural hair colour. A small vanity I told myself; women do it all the time. I believe now that it was an indicator of his true character, that and all his shoes were slip-ons, every single pair.

He was courteous in small things like closing the door after I got into the passenger seat of his car and helping me on with my coat. I was flattered he found me interesting. We began a relationship – I hadn't always been so cautious.

He often talked about administering the website.

'The beauty is that I can be anywhere,' he said. 'I could be answering a query about how to get mayonnaise off a tablecloth sitting in the south of France. Oh, yes. I like the thought of that.'

He leaned back in his chair and flipped some crumbs off his tie. We were in the café opposite the multi-storey car park in Leatherhead following a presentation on home-made cleaning products. It was raining.

'You get real quality of life down there – weather can't be beaten. Think of everyone slogging away in the UK. That's where we should be – soaking up the sun.'

'Do you mean it?' I asked him.

'I'm a serious man, Alison. Question is, can you leave all this behind?'

He gestured towards the dull street. I laughed.

'Course I could.'

'What about Neil?' he said, toying with the white minaret lid of the salt cellar.

We didn't often talk about my son. Neil was not a fan of William.

'He'll be off on his own soon,' I said.

'The language wouldn't bother you?'

'It wouldn't matter if I was with you. I could do it.'

'Yes, I think you might.'

William approved a shortlist of properties that had online details. I whittled them down on my own, travelling by train to the south of France. Three weeks later I was in negotiations. I had arranged a second mortgage in the UK to provide the capital, but everything was more expensive than I'd imagined. I admitted this to the agent immobilier and he had introduced me to the local bank manager who quickly arranged a loan. They fussed over having everything translated, made sure I was guided through all the unfamiliar processes.

'There's always hidden costs, Alison,' said William when I told him. 'Don't worry so much. It's still a bargain.'

'It won't leave very much.'

'Think what you can do with the garden. Come here, give us a cuddle.' He placed his finger on the tip of my nose and winked. 'You're one in a million.'

When I told him the house sale had gone through with the notary he laughed.

'It's not really ready to move into,' I said. 'The upstairs shower leaks and there's bound to be other things. I'm afraid I'm going to need more money.'

'You'll get it all sorted.'

'And Neil needs to pay his course fees.'

'How old is he now? It wouldn't do him any harm to get a job,' he said. 'Why don't you sell this place?'

'I thought about renting it out?'

'No, there won't be much interest in this kind of place. Not without updating. Why do you want to keep it?'

'I hadn't…do you really think so?'

Neil took it personally when the house went on the market. I told him I was moving on, that William and I had a future together. He disagreed.

Strangers strolled around the living room on sunny afternoons stealing glances at our old family photographs; many included Neil's father before he died. I didn't like that.

At the same time invoices were coming through from France, first from the plumber and then the electrician – who'd been called by the plumber after he accidentally disconnected the heating thermostat.

The first instalment of the French loan became due. I dropped the price of the house to make a sale. When I received the money William persuaded me to invest in the website. He said he'd pay me for blogging and answering questions on the noticeboard. He said doing it through the company would save me paying tax.

My possessions were wrapped, stacked and sealed into cartons. They were put into a storage warehouse just outside Reading until the French house was ready.

I arrived at twenty-seven bis Rue St Joseph late one night with three suitcases. It was the middle of March and bitterly cold.

Inside there were puddles of water beneath many of the tall windows. In one bedroom a chunk of plasterwork had fallen to the floor and lay in a sodden pile of paint-splinters on the wooden boards. There was no electricity or running water.

A local man who worked the allotment between the back of the house and the river offered his services for building work and renovating the garden. A sustained assault was necessary before I could do anything outside – the garden was infested with creeping buttercup, convolvulus and briars. I agreed to pay him a small monthly salary. He took the money for little or no work until one day in autumn when he turned up, said he wouldn't be able to finish the job, apologised half-heartedly and left.

I see him occasionally at the Wednesday market drinking Pastis behind a grubby stall where he sells fresh produce. He has had a fine harvest of squashes, beans, potatoes and all sorts of other root vegetables. I have grown nothing.

I do my shopping in the supermarché, cruising entire aisles

devoted to cheese and cold meat. I pick up packets briskly then decipher labels at home. It takes a week to get through a packet of sliced meat on my own.

I stare longest at the shelves of cleaning products where trial and error is more expensive. There is half an aisle devoted to the care and maintenance of tiled floors. The local word is 'carrelage'. It's the only practical surface here in the summer and quite standard. I yearn for carpet on cold days.

Yesterday, while I gazed at the colourful array of spray-on cleaners, the woman next to me took a tall red bottle from the shelf. She had tanned arms and wore a fitted black dress. A blonde ponytail lay smoothly down her back. I copied her and took one for myself. I became self-conscious of my hands, their knuckles like elephant's knees and the short pale-grey nails. She said something encouraging in French nodding at the bottle then she sighed and patted me on the shoulder. I suddenly found myself on the verge of tears. I crept closer to the shelves and stood pretending to read the instructions until she was gone.

There are days I long to talk. I have to force myself not to prolong the simple exchange of courtesies at the till in order not to look ridiculous.

When I first arrived and was hopeful, gleeful at my new position, I would order coffee at Café Rose and sit by the river at my own little table. I amused myself by imagining the conversations William and I would have while looking over at the old house with lilac shutters. I had no intimation that one day I would be preparing myself for an interview with its owner, Monsieur Lenoir.

The loan repayments had quickly emptied what was left in my savings account and I was running short of money for day to day living expenses when William revealed his hand.

'When are you coming?' I said. 'Have you booked your ticket for the twenty-third?'

'How's the building work?' he replied.

'I'm not sure the builder understands what I want done, but he says he needs paying some sort of advance. Can you put some money in my account?'

'I wish I could, but it wouldn't look right on the books –

there haven't been any posts on your blog recently. Really, Alison, I could do with more input at this stage.'

'But you know I'm busy with the house,' I said.

'Things are taking off here. I've got companies interested in advertising, we're linking up with other sites.'

'Why don't you just come and work here?'

'You're not on-line yet.'

'No. It's a bit of a battle actually.'

'How fast's the connection for data streaming?'

'The what? They say they're coming as soon as they can.'

'I need to be hands on at this point. I can't afford to be out of the loop.'

'William, you told me that you wanted to be here.'

'I never *told* you to do anything,' he said.

'You said I should go! And now, why won't you come?'

'Don't push me, Annie.'

'Who's Annie?'

'Sorry, Alison, a slip of the tongue. Listen, I'll be honest… things are moving on here. I mean, there's more than one way to get grease stains off lampshade covers.'

'What? What are you talking about? You know I can't afford this on my own. I need my investment money back.'

'It's all tied up for the moment. You'll find a way to manage. I need to be making contacts.'

'I don't see ho–'

'I've got to go. There's a call on the mobile,' said William. 'You need to stand on your own two feet, Ann…Alison.'

It was after the second slip I became suspicious. There was another month of calls that never achieved anything. Finally, he told me.

'Listen. Alison, I can see you're too busy to carry on the blog. Have you seen the new 'Annie's answers' link? It's very popular. I've been helping her get started. Truth is, we've become close…'

I hung up. I didn't wait for more.

How could I have been so blind? So stupid? Why didn't I listen to Neil?

There are some days when nothing, nothing except my solitude, which I wrap like brown paper around my shame, keeps me from putting an end to it all.

For the interview I choose a corduroy skirt, a cream shirt and red cardigan. If William saw me again he might be surprised. My waist and hips *had* softened and spread with menopause, but the events of the last year have slowed and reversed this thickening. I am slim, sun-bronzed.

It is cool today; the summer heat has passed. Everything echoes in the empty air of the house as I get ready to leave.

I anticipate that Monsieur Lenoir knows who I am – the English woman who lives alone on Rue St Joseph – but I know nothing of him.

I arrive at the time we arranged on the telephone. He is frail, wearing a cardigan and slippers. His head rests forward slightly, bringing his ears level with angular wing-like shoulders. It became clear on the phone that his English is as poor as my French. We quickly resort to using our native languages and gestures. After ten minutes he writes a sum on a piece of paper. I nod my head.

I am taken on a tour of the house. Monsieur Lenoir goes before me. The first flight of stairs is broad with shallow steps and a simple balustrade. The wood is dark, like all the wood in the house, smoothed by countless hands and feet. I know before I take the first tread that each step will have a signature creak.

On the first floor there is a bathroom with white rectangular tiles arranged lengthways that remind me of an underground station. There are also two bedrooms, one barely large enough for a double bed; the other is furnished grandly with a marble fireplace.

The second set of stairs is as narrow as a tea-tray, gloomily lit by a high window. The rooms above cut into the eaves. There is a bathroom with sink, bidet and toilet, and two bedrooms identical in size with round windows like portholes. Each is furnished with a small bed and a table. He takes me into one of the rooms, on the table there is an ewer and basin like you might see for sale on the brocante stalls, the smudged yellow flowers worn away with use. On the floor beneath there is a matching chamber pot containing two dead flies.

The last flight of stairs corkscrews vertically upwards. I hold the rail tightly as I ascend. There is barely enough room for two people on the landing. Monsieur Lenoir pauses for breath and clears his throat. There is a single door.

'Voilà Madame,' he says, injecting a flourish into his worn out voice.

The door swings open and there is a deluge of light and warmth. I walk into a glass-walled room in which every colour is fiercely strong; vibrant orange, electric purple, brilliant red and pure sunshine yellow. The citron smell of geranium and soft sweetness of marigold suffuses the air. A round table and two delicate ornate metal chairs rest in the centre of this miniature Eden. My imagination adds the sounds of birdsong and dripping water.

I don't know what my new employer is saying; something about flowers perhaps? He makes a watering gesture, demonstrates opening and closing the windows with cords to clarify understanding of my duties here.

I walk over to the glass wall and look down. Below me is the café. Most of the tables are empty, but I can see two women, one older, one younger. The younger has striking chestnut hair. She drinks her coffee slowly and is looking at the lilac shutters.

I turn around and look into the bright red of the geranium petals. They are so red it almost hurts, it blots out my thoughts leaving behind nothing but red.

'Ça va, Madame?'

'Oui. Oui, merci.'

The tour is over. The mood in this airborne greenhouse is so different from the rest of the house. I sense, that if I know how to take it, there may be the opportunity here for a better new beginning.

A Good Hiding

'I remember your father hitting you across the back of the legs – he left a mark. I don't know what you had done.'

My aunt's voice is calm; her tone betrays no condemnation. The comment is made humorously more than anything else.

'I don't remember,' I say.

'It was after,' she says.

The sentence hangs in the air.

I know I was smacked, but I have no recollection of the incident she refers to. In fact my memories of early childhood are so fragmented there never seems anything worth looking back on. Not until I went to live with Aunt Cecilia do events hang together in any sort of logical order.

Today we are sitting together outside Café Rose. On our right there is the river, dark and green, bending the light into convex ripples. I sip my coffee and look onto the square. I want to add another cube of sugar, but I resist and try to savour the unfamiliar bitter-rich flavour.

Cecilia doesn't know this may be our last holiday together; there is going to be change. She doesn't drink coffee. She swirls her pot of tea, tuts at the straw-coloured liquid flowing from the spout then adds a generous slop of milk into the cup. We relapse into silence and watch the filling tables.

My father – who I've not seen for over a year – takes his tea strong with two heaped teaspoons of sugar. Running out of tea or sugar puts him in an irreconcilable temper. Even though he lives on his own I've noticed he buys increasingly large packets of both; bulk-buy boxes of two-hundred tea bags and kilos of granulated sugar line the back of the cupboard above the kettle. I'm not sure whether it is forethought or economy. Sometimes – I don't know why – I think it is a sign of regret. He has no other self-indulgences left that I know of; cigarettes went a decade ago, whisky – watered down to almost nothing – is only taken once a night, and food – I don't think he notices what he eats at all.

I take another sip of coffee, it's warming on this overcast afternoon. Earlier, after a slow walk around the rose garden and fountain, including an examination of the statue of a local martyred Abbé, we had browsed leaflets and maps in the Office de Tourisme and made plans while walking to the square. Mist hangs around the steep hillsides. Light rain has come and gone all day. There is a lethargic mood around the country town.

All of a sudden I recall a moment from my childhood. Maybe it's because I'm so far removed from my usual surroundings that the memory feels extraordinarily vivid – like an inoculation – an injection piercing the present.

It's an ordinary day. I'm lying on the steps looking at the kitchen floor tiles. They are small and square with a pattern of brown and white flowers. I used to marvel at how the flowers transformed into geometric patterns. I can see the gate-leg table, the veneer top peeling off in one corner. I see the gas boiler. It clicks and the pilot light ignites as it did every night; if I peeked under the table I would see the small blue flame. There's a spider plant on the new fridge with Kamikaze offspring trailing over the side.

All of this I see in an instant. It's as familiar as my face in the mirror.

My eye level is the same height as the worktop where spoons and knives and mixing bowls are just within my reach. Like today it is also grey and wet outside – not the type of day I would usually go out and play. Despite what I said when people asked me later, I preferred to be inside with mum even with the new baby crying.

My grandmother used to say, 'That baby saved your life. And to think everyone used to complain about its crying,' then she'd fussily fold her cardigan over her chest. It was her sign for no more talking. She was a plain speaker, a trait passed on to my father.

Cecilia tries to be the same, but she is softer. Occasional fancies take hold of her. I remember her being determined to toast marshmallows one bonfire night. We had no place for a bonfire, no neighbours who invited us over, so we toasted them through the grill of the gas fire. As Cecilia stretched pink marshmallow from the drooping blob on her fork she had exclaimed, 'What would your mother say!' She looked at me and smiled, licked her fingers and offered me another. The caramelised exterior fizzled on our saliva. The next morning I queued for communion with numb patches on my tongue where it had been scalded the night before.

We regularly did things together my aunt and I, even when I was very young. So it was natural I would want to live with her. We've similar tastes in a number of things.

Sometimes I see physical similarities between her and my father. She has handsome features; long-faced, sallow-skinned with aquamarine eyes; when she was younger she had luxurious chestnut-coloured hair. I can't help wondering how her life could have been different, but to even discuss it would break another family taboo.

I notice Cecilia's gaze resting on a small window box layered with red geraniums and blue lobelia. There are lilac shutters either side of the window, each differently crooked. They are around all the upper windows of this old house that looks onto the square.

There were geraniums in our garden when I was young; none brilliant red like these, more a mix of salmon-pink and acid-orange. They grew near the prickly mahonia that – unable to resist their highly scented yellow petals – I stripped of flowers each February.

I would pick whatever was in flower. I found the glow of flower heads against cool green leaves irresistible. Even daisies I would pluck by the dozen from the lawn, until my skirt was full and the lawn reduced to a pool of green.

I'm certain my father never particularly cared about my flower-beheading misdemeanours, but he overreacted to any action he saw as wilful naughtiness. The problem was that I could never be discreet about my floral treasure. I displayed it in cups, on bricks, along lines of paving stones. I decorated the divide between the neat square of mown grass and the wilder thicket beyond where I could make myself entirely disappear. I can remember my mother and the neighbours calling and calling my name thinking me lost. I would be at the end of that long thin garden, but I never came out until I heard my father calling when he came home. I knew then the game was up.

'Mary-Ellen! Come out now if you know what's good for you!'

There was rarely anything good waiting for me – if I believed I had a reason to hide I was usually right.

The lilac shutters, there is something about them, an iridescence despite the mid-afternoon gloom, that brings to my mind the eye of the cooker's gas flame in the old kitchen. I am taken back to watching the crown of flames fluttering under a small silver pan. I couldn't see – but I knew that the pan was half-filled with water and balanced inside was a jar of baby food set to warm. I had heard the scrape-pop of the lid being removed and watched my mother turn gas flame low.

She was distracted. The crying baby was now able to roll and was banging its head against the wooden legs of the dining chairs. The gas spluttered in the draught of air from my mother's quick turn. The buds of flame rippled then disappeared completely leaving blank eyelets around a flat black disc. The baby was picked up and the crying subsided to more deliberate sobbing.

I reached out to the worn dial and moved it around a quarter-inch until the gas was switched off. The soft hiss from the ring quietened.

Later, my father came in and saw the bruise on the crying baby's head.

'Don't you keep an eye on him?'

'You won't believe how much he moves around. There's not enough space in here.'

'Why's all this stuff lying around?'

'I was having a clear out.'

'Where's Mary-Ellen?'

'In the kitchen, the garden maybe. I don't know.'

I had been leaning against the back door listening, but when I heard this I went outside.

On the terrace of Café Rose my coffee has cooled, still warm, but no longer as satisfying. I add another sugar cube in a moment of self-indulgence and enjoy the over-sweet second half of the cup.

The next morning Cecilia and I walk around the market. There is a rotisserie, stalls of local cheese and fresh produce as well as a few clothes and household items. We browse for a while then move to the tables displaying *brocante* – the local word for antiques/bric-a-brac.

Three stallholders are gathered around the back of an open minivan. There is a table between them with crusty bread and a dish of white and yellow cheese. A bottle of rosé wine, still misted, is being poured into plastic beakers. I imagine the smell of alcohol on their breath in the afternoon as they try to sell three-legged stools and lace.

I stare at a rose-decorated chamber pot and remember a dim room, the curtains drawn in summertime, and my father coming in and kneeling at my bedside. He places a hand on my shoulder.

'I'm sorry,' he says. 'I didn't mean it. I was just angry. Let's be friends again. Come on Mary-Ellen. Are you awake? I know you're awake. Don't ignore me. Say you'll forget all about it. Hmm…won't you?' He exhales. 'Don't be like this. I didn't mean it. Let's be friends. Come on. Look at me won't you?'

His breath is laden with alcohol. There's a trace of sweetness, like Ovaltine, but mostly it's a bitter horrid smell. I don't like it. I want him to go away. I don't want his apology, not now. I'm tired. I don't know why he won't go away. Aren't I pretending well enough to be asleep? Surely he knows I'm pretending. Get the hint. Go away. I'm not going to open my eyes. I'm not.

'Come on Mary, don't be like this.'

He bends over, kind of hugs me by the shoulders and kisses me on the cheek. I hold my breath, and hold it and hold it and hold it until he's gone and has shut the door. Then I turn my face into my pillow. My breaths turn to sobs. I can't help it. I didn't want his stupid apology.

'Madame, c'est quatorze euro.'

The store holder gestures at the porcelain bowl.

'What? I mean, pardon? Non, merci.'

We move on. Cecilia touches the spines of second-hand books, turns her head to look at their titles, but I'm distracted now. I don't have patience for the overpriced knick-knacks. They are charmless, made more so by the overflowing bins and broken-up surface of the car park where the market is held.

It isn't often that I think back to the event that led my father and I to move away from that house – there was no question of our staying. My grandmother took me back to collect a few things, but most items were abandoned; my mother's clothes, the baby's cot blankets and teddy bear. Everything not already destroyed was soon buried during demolition.

My father became unreliable. I lived with my grandmother briefly, then it was decided that I would go and live with Cecilia on my own.

His apologies always came late at night after a few drinks, whenever we were under the same roof. When I became a teenager I was allowed a lock on my door. Although I never used it when only Cecilia and I were in the house I would slip the catch when I heard his footsteps on the stairs. The apologising stopped; his visits became less frequent.

Cecilia interrupts my train of thought.

'Isn't it lovely? Of course, we'd never get it home unbroken.'

The mirror has a gilt frame, coils of foliage and flowers blossoming and drooping over the glass. The silver is tarnished; golden spots and streaks mar the reflection.

'C'est combien?' I ask.

'Trente-cinq euros.'

The stallholder is female with black frizzy hair, skinny arms and a voice coarsened by decades of smoking. I translate for Cecilia and then reply.

'Non, merci.'

'It's a shame. We could do with something like that in the hall,' says Cecilia, 'but not at that price.'

My reflection grows more and more like the memory I have of my mother. Next year I will be the age she was when the accident happened. In September Cecilia and I will visit her grave and leave flowers; one for my mother and a similar smaller bunch for the baby. They have matching dates of death, perhaps not so unusual in older areas of the churchyard, but they are singular in the modern expansion of God's Little Acre for the identical date of death; perhaps identical in moment as well.

She was always forgetful or distracted my mother. I loved it most when she held me in her arms, kissing and tickling close

13

under my ear. Little things never seemed to matter when it was me and her and the baby – who cried a lot.

When the explosion happened it's likely they were in each other's arms – impossible though to shield a baby from the blast.

Gas had filled the kitchen. It was ignited when the boiler's timer clicked around. The automatic pilot light mechanism created a spark to ignite the flame – to heat the water for my bath.

Once I understood how it worked I'd got into the habit of checking the stove, watching the flames, hearing the hiss. Quite often I'd made it safe. But the day before the accident my father had been there. *He had seen me turn the dial and he had told me off.* So that last day, even though he was not there, I decided to leave it alone. I went instead to the very, very end of the garden where you couldn't hear anything at all from inside the house.

'Attention, Madame!'

A car horn blares out at me. Cecilia is grasping my arm. She thanks the bystander in English, shaking then nodding her head.

'Take care! Remember "adroit",' she says – pronouncing the 't'. 'Remember "adroit". Oh, Ellen, you gave me a fright.'

We walk on. I apologise for my carelessness.

I have planned for us to have lunch at the café. Today, I will tell Cecilia that I have put a deposit on a flat in town. When we return I will be moving in with someone I have been seeing, someone who I think I am in love with. One of the many things I have learned from Cecilia is how to explain things – and to believe I am lovable.

Brocante

Monsieur Lenoir wrote the notice in capital letters. It read, somewhat shakily, 'HELP WANTED FOR GENERAL CLEANING DUTIES. ENQUIRE WITHIN.' The postcard-sized advertisement rested on the glass of the ground floor window facing Café Rose. He removed it every Saturday, Tuesday and Thursday evening before his daughter Sylvia arrived from Toulouse. Perhaps it was because of this that there were no enquiries into the position for some time.

Sylvia would be cross if she found out his plan. Recently she had begun turning the conversation toward selling the house and finding something more practical. She had begun bringing back boxes from the supermarché, packing family photographs and keepsakes. He noticed that the boxes had once held cans of iced tea. Monsieur Lenoir had taken a fancy to trying the drink after seeing a young man sipping it on the terrace of the café. He found it excessively sweet; the artificial aftertaste of peaches lingered on his tongue.

Monsieur Lenoir was not such a fool as to believe it was simply the beverage he was drawn to; his life had grown solitary. Dust and memories piled up in the house.

His only son Patrick had died when only a young man, on a stretch of road near Nébias. Straight as an arrow the road dipped in and out of the shadows of the plane trees, which prevented the tarmac melting in summer. The Municipal Police estimated that Patrick had been going a hundred kilometres an hour, not excessive for such a stretch, when a pigeon collided with his motorcycle helmet.

Patrick's chin flipped upwards, his neck broken. He was killed as instantly as the bird. There were plenty of other broken bones, some from being wrenched from the motorbike, others from a secondary collision with a Peugeot travelling behind. The couple in it had no time to react, hardly had time to see what happened. They told Monsieur Lenoir later, 'It was like a dream. The bird flying out of the shade into the sun. There was no chance to avoid it.'

Monsieur Lenoir mused bitterly to himself in the weeks that followed. 'My only son, my dear son – killed by a pigeon.'

He imagined children in the local playground chanting, 'Patrick met a pigeon, a pigeon, a pigeon. Patrick met a pigeon, a pigeon, a pigeon met he…' dancing, holding hands, laughing gleefully at the silliness of it all. So was this his tragedy? Perhaps not. There was his marriage to Audrey, although calling the marriage a tragedy over-dramatised what he knew was a mistake in judgement. Her long pale-brown hair, curling lashes and eyes the colour of chocolate drops gave the impression of feminine softness. Yet, when he saw her eyes slide sideways he knew she was about to get down to business.

He'd never particularly desired a wife, but he'd wanted children. Their courtship had taken place in the wake of the completion of his national service. Here he had thrived, surrounded by camaraderie and the blank easy happiness of shared physical exertion. In self-indulgent moments Monsieur Lenoir re-created in his mind the details of a particular warm afternoon spent swimming in the Canal du Midi with members of his company; each leaf; each ripple. They had lain on the bank to dry, sometimes waving to passing boats. Passengers toasted their discarded uniforms, others whistled at the sight of their white skin against suntanned necks and arms. He remembered a cluster of cornflowers in an old kettle, drifting past on the prow of a barge.

Sylvia had been born a year after his marriage. The baby's arrival distracted Audrey from his deficiencies.

His wife's practical entrepreneurial nature flourished running the business they had taken over from her father. They supplied shops and restaurants with fresh meat, fruit and vegetables from local producers. Audrey negotiated low prices, promising repeat business to the farmers, he made the deliveries. The profits soon enabled them to make a down payment on a house.

'Look at the portholes,' she told him, in a moment of imagination, 'just like a ship's. We'll have the children's rooms at the top.'

'We only have Sylvia,' he'd replied.

'Surely you want a son, Monsieur Lenoir!'

She chuckled, pinched his cheek then crossed the street to begin haggling with the agent. By the time negotiations concluded the price had been cut by twenty-percent and new pipe work and the conversion of a small roof terrace to a sunroom were included.

Dutifully, he fulfilled her ambition for him to have a son. Patrick was born without difficulty on a dank morning in November. Audrey agreed afterwards, without great discussion or the need for persuasion, that it would be sensible not to have any more children. His virility left him, he felt alone and surrounded by the rising water of defeat.

One morning nearly forty years later, whilst energetically buffing the carrelage – a job she would never consider trusting to a stranger – Audrey collapsed. She lingered in her bed for a week during which she recommended Monsieur Lenoir to Sylvia's care. There had been no consultation with him in the matter. The next morning, almost as if she had said to herself, 'Well this isn't much of a life is it?' she died.

Like the afternoon on the canal Monsieur Lenoir remembered the day precisely. He remembered staring at his wife's hands. Lined with blue and purple, dotted with faded moles and growing skin spots, they matched his own. A long sigh drew out of him.

Sylvia, who had always fussed over the condition of the house when Audrey was alive, lost interest in its gloomy rooms and the charms of its historic plasterwork.

One morning on her return from the boulangerie she announced, 'I'm moving.'

'Moving?'

Sylvia laid the baguette on the table.

'I've negotiated a good price on an old town house. It needs fixing up, but I don't mind the work.'

'A town house?'

'In Toulouse.'

'You don't know anyone in Toulouse.'

'I'll get to know the town soon enough. I'll need help with the advance.'

Monsieur Lenoir gave Sylvia the money. She left the following month. He heard exploits of the house renovations, about lodgers and friends and the new neighbourhood. It was vibrant, she said, with a mixture of cultures and nationalities. Despite her conservatism Sylvia thrived. Like an old stone on a riverbed Monsieur Lenoir never went to see the town house. It was enough that the place existed and his daughter seemed happy. Her return visits were spent efficiently tidying, cleaning and preparing meals, but they had little to talk about.

One afternoon in late spring he received a phone call. Sylvia told him she had slipped while re-grouting tiles in the bathroom and would not be visiting for at least a fortnight. He assured her that he would manage. The timing was fortuitous – he had at last received an application for the cleaning position.

Something of interest was also happening in the Café Rose. There was activity inside the windows. The tired pink curtains had been replaced by draped material of primrose yellow. The plastic table covers, secured by rusted metal clips were removed, replaced by red and white gingham. On Friday evening an artist's easel supporting a large menu board appeared outside. Monsieur Lenoir paused on his walk to the boulodrome. The fountain's droplets, swept by the breeze, lightly tickled his skin as he read.

'Chef Jean has taken over at Café Rose and invites you to sample his menu, 15 euros. Book early!' A list of suggestions followed; nothing over embellished, just simple dishes accented with herbs, garlic and lemon, rich in butter and cream.

It would certainly be preferable to anything he cooked for himself or bought from the counter at the supermarché. Monsieur Lenoir reserved a table. He waited with anticipation for evening time.

In retrospect he couldn't have said exactly why he enjoyed the food so much, but when the chef appeared to meet his customers Monsieur Lenoir was determined to shower him with high praise.

Jean was in his early forties – a young man to Monsieur Lenoir's eyes – slim and athletic looking. He frequently wore a maroon baseball cap, an item Monsieur Lenoir disliked, yet on the chef he saw it as appropriate – no doubt practical in the kitchen. Jean emerged after dessert wearing a closely fitting white t-shirt and a small apron tied around his hips. He greeted Monsieur Lenoir.

Monsieur Lenoir found himself blushing.

'The food…it's superb. I don't know when I've eaten better.'

'The compliment is too much. Thank you. I believe I have the pleasure of being opposite your house, Monsieur.'

'Well my wife, she decided on it. But she's dead now. I am in the house alone. I'm glad you like it, what with us being neighbours. The glass room at the top – you see above the portholes – that's my special place. One time you must come up and see the view of the café.'

'That's very kind, Monsieur. I'm pleased you enjoyed your meal. If you will excuse me, I have to keep doing the rounds.'

Jean patted Monsieur Lenoir on the shoulder then walked away. A simple friendly gesture, but it stirred him somehow.

The next day Monsieur Lenoir used cologne after shaving, disciplined his grey hair with oil, chose a clean shirt and contrived to wait until ten-thirty before arriving at the Café Rose for coffee. He took a table near the river, away from the bustle of the Wednesday market in the square. Immediately he wished he'd chosen a different seat, one where he might see more into the interior of the café. A yawning Clotilde Lentier took his order.

'Un café, s'il vous plait.'

From then on Monsieur Lenoir's morning coffee at the café became a steady habit. Sylvia, busy enjoying her second youth, approved of his taking meals there and to his surprise made no opposition to the employment of a cleaning lady.

He nurtured the familiarity that grew with Jean although to some it seemed plain there was little in common between them. Monsieur Lenoir watched the chef talking with the customers and occasionally serving tables when Clotilde was away. Jean complained how the waitress was always having dramas with her children who stayed at home all day while she worked.

If you had asked Monsieur Lenoir if he was happy during this time he would have replied, 'Yes.' That he was an old man whose knees ached in cold weather, whose sole remaining child was increasingly aloof, and who had neither means nor inclination to prepare his house for approaching infirmity, wouldn't have influenced his answer.

The morning, moist and scented, provided incentive enough to rise. His visit to the café punctuated the time before lunch. In the afternoon he might watch boules, after which he would rest, then it would be evening and more often than not dinner at the café.

He felt youthful. His strength seemed to return the more time he spent at the café. It didn't occur to Monsieur Lenoir that he wanted more than Jean's cooking and pleasant conversation until one afternoon in June.

It had been unusually hot for early summer. Each day the thermometer in Monsieur Lenoir's rooftop greenhouse read above thirty-five degrees. The cleaning lady had re-positioned a variegated specimen by the window. Its needle like hairs broke open as she brushed against the drooping stems and released a fresh green scent into the sweltering glass cubicle. The geranium greedily sucked up the water she poured.

Monsieur Lenoir stood, one hand gripping his cane, watching the café below. Beneath them Jean was speaking to a newcomer to the town, smiling, nodding his head, gesturing with open hands.

The man was recently arrived by motorcycle. A thick-wheeled machine, with practically an armchair for a seat and two bulky panniers strapped to either side. In Monsieur Lenoir's opinion it was a ridiculous machine; a vehicle singularly incapable of adventure. He watched Jean desert his afternoon customers and be led over to view the hunk of metal. It leaned heavily on its stand like a fat man on a stool.

There was something about how Jean's hand rested on the seat where the newcomer had so recently sat, the way his index finger traced the curve of the handlebars, that made Monsieur Lenoir hate the rider of this two-wheeled monster. There was nothing special about the newcomer to his eyes. He was of medium height with mousey hair, medium in everything in fact. It was impossible to conjecture what sort of body was beneath the padded jacket and trousers.

Jean however, smiled and ushered the man back towards the café. The chef disappeared for a moment then came back balancing a beer in a stemmed glass on a tray. He rested the drink on the table and placed his hand on the newcomer's shoulder.

At that moment Monsieur Lenoir discovered his capacity for passion was intact. He was not a doormat or a wet blanket, as his father used to call him. Yes, he was gentle and circumspect; there was nothing wrong with that. But there were limits.

Monsieur Lenoir turned away from the scene and began to descend the stairs. He had decided to act, but he would wait until the cleaning woman had gone. It was Friday and she had set to with bleach in the hardly used bathrooms. He patiently listened to her shake and re-make the beds. When she had finished she approached where he sat in the kitchen.

Her French was improving slowly.

'C'est tout?' she said.

'Oui.'

He motioned for her to wait then said in English.

'Do you like the house?'

'Yes.'

'It is not too big for you to look after?'

'No.'

'You like the plants?'

'Yes. It's a lot of stairs, but such a cheerful bright place.'

He nodded and wished her good day. When she had gone he entered Audrey's study and took a sheet of paper from her bureau. He wrote a few lines then placed it in an envelope addressed to the town notary Monsieur Demain. He paused then filled out a cheque for the costs of changing his will.

'Maintenant,' he muttered to himself.

He took a bunch of keys from the top drawer and walked over to the glass cabinet on the wall; a gun case left to him by his father. When Monsieur Lenoir had baulked at military service his father had said briskly, 'A man should know how to use a weapon.'

In the end Monsieur Lenoir had become a more than adequate marksman.

The lock turned with crafted smoothness and he lifted the gun. He'd forgotten the weight of the weapon and the heavy metal barrel almost slipped from his grasp. He left his stick resting in the study, took small careful steps until he reached the banister. When he reached the top of the last staircase his heart was racing.

Fragrance surrounded him in the humid glass-walled room. Outside the motorcycle was in the same place. Café Rose was quiet. To an onlooker nothing had changed. Monsieur Lenoir watched. He practised raising the pistol, releasing the safety catch and taking aim.

Where was Jean?

Monsieur Lenoir remembered the signs. Intuition told him that this afternoon Jean was not working in the kitchen; he was in the apartment on the first floor.

What was he doing?

Monsieur Lenoir picked off the crispy dead petals from a tired geranium and waited. He sighed. If only he'd had a little more time. Sure, he didn't have much to offer. But he'd thought perhaps Jean might want to make him happy.

At five o'clock the temperature was still hot. A gusty wind swirled down from the Pyrenees. Jean stepped onto his balcony. He lit a cigarette, called over his shoulder and passed it from his mouth to the outstretched hand of the newcomer. The man received the cigarette without pause or thanks. He'd removed all his motorcycle clothing and had flushed cheeks. Jean glanced upwards to the window of the glass room. Monsieur Lenoir raised his hand in acknowledgement then took a step backwards. The moment had come. As he pulled off the safety catch he thought, 'A man should know how to use a weapon.' If he didn't then what sort of man was he?

His action wouldn't have been a surprise to those young men on the canal bank. Amongst them were those who understood, who'd experienced the same jealousies and delights.

Everyone in town was astonished by the shot.

Banging and Screaming

Clotilde trailed the car keys along the table then clasped them in her hand.

'Your sister owes me after this.'

'What time did she call?' said Linette.

'Four something, I don't know,' said Clotilde. 'What time is it now?'

'Five-fifteen.'

Linette removed her hand from the kettle. She would rather head back to bed than talk to her mother.

'At least it's Saturday,' said Clotilde. 'Look after Diane. Give her some breakfast.'

Linette nodded.

The mirror by the door was dark, but Clotilde still pushed back her hair and pursed her lips.

Ève had never done this before, although she'd done plenty of other things. Once, she'd taken the car without asking and arrived back at one o'clock in the morning. They'd set to with an argument in the car park.

Monsieur Claude had yelled down from his balcony.

'Shut up down there! I'm trying to sleep.'

Ève and Clotilde stopped shouting at each other and gave him what for.

'You miserable old git,' called Ève. 'Can't you see this is a personal affair? Pull your head in and get back to your filthy poker.'

'You little slut! Like mother like daugh–'

'Don't talk to my daughter like that,' shouted Clotilde. 'Bald headed fool, nobody would touch you with a barge pole.'

'Slut!'

'Come down here and say that!'

Lights went on; several other shutters wound up. Madame Delecriox' baby started bawling. They knew it wouldn't be long before Monsieur Fitou called his nephew at the municipal police. Clotilde had shouted, 'Fuck-off' half a dozen times at the windows then yelled at the empty street for good measure before going inside and slamming the door.

When they got into the flat Clotilde and Ève had drunk the bottle of Blanquette they'd been given by the pawnbrokers at Christmas. Everything had been forgiven.

Even now, setting off before dawn groggy and angry, Clotilde knew it was unlikely she would be furious with Ève for long. Linette was a different matter, Linette with her petty grievances, *'Who ate the last vanilla pudding?'* etc. etc. The very sight of her could make Clotilde mad for days on end. Yes, Linette had a mean streak in her, something unbending; something quite cold.

Despite this, Clotilde had never made Linette clear out. She wasn't yet sixteen anyway, and she kept an eye on Diane while Clotilde worked. Clotilde trusted her more than Jacques, but that wasn't saying much.

Linette and Jacques' father had moved to Spain when Clotilde told him she was pregnant a second time. Ève had been upset when he left. She'd been old enough to become attached to the man who brought chocolate bars and Disney magazines every time he wanted to stay the night. Clotilde had known all along he was a bastard.

Clotilde paused by the car, stretching her arms above her head. She could smell cigarette smoke. The lights were on in Madame Crébor's living room. She would already have the television on and her first glass of Pastis by her elbow. A yellow stray mewed impatiently at the old woman's doorway.

The journey to Toulouse would take nearly two hours. The road followed the limestone cliffs of the gorge, passing through sharp-cornered villages with narrow streets. It was impossible to speed. Most of the settlements were half-deserted; no one wanted to live in old houses anymore, not if they had a choice.

The flat was better, not that she kept it spotless, but at least everything worked. If it didn't, or if something got broken, she just had to tell the housing department to send someone over.

The petrol light flickered on.

'Shit.'

She knew it would be a close thing.

An ambulance car whizzed past her at St Jean de Fleurs, narrowly avoiding an oncoming truck. It would be unlucky to have a collision at this time, but it did happen.

Out of the gorge on the plains, the bone white tree trunks stood out against the petrol blue sky; it wasn't long before the flat shadows of dawn came into focus. Clotilde had seen plenty of early mornings for one reason or another. They had nearly been the last straw when Diane was a baby. The pregnancy had come after a one-night stand with a guy who sold second-hand clothes at the Wednesday market.

She had been pretty sure it was him, and she'd been proved right. Diane was the colour of a kidney bean when she was born. Shiny and wet, her skin had been like cocoa against Clotilde's rice-pudding coloured breasts.

Clotilde hadn't known how to fix Diane's hair until a Cameroonian woman moved into the flat below. Angelique had braided and oiled Diane's hair while Clotilde filled their glasses and they talked away the afternoons.

Angelique had a twisted hip that hadn't fixed properly following a car accident in her childhood. Clotilde had helped her claim disability benefit.

'There was nothing to see,' said Angelique. 'But every day it was crunching inside when I walked, like a cat chewing up bones. My mother kept saying, "Why can't you walk straight, girl?" She took me to the local man who tried to pull it into place. She held me down while he pulled, yanking me this way and that. Oh, I screamed and hollered, holding onto the handles of that bed. I never knew pain before he did all that. Afterwards, I made myself always walk straight. I didn't complain about any pain. Bought my own medicine and put up with it. My God, the things I do. I don't think I'll ever stop taking those medicines. Too used to them now.' Angelique would pat Diane's hair. 'Isn't she beautiful? Eh, Clotilde? He must have been handsome enough. Look at that shine on her skin!'

'Yes, handsome enough,' said Clotilde.

Clotilde had raised her glass and admired her daughter. She'd wondered if there would be more to Diane than her other girls.

Clotilde's ribs rubbed against the car door as she snatched the ticket from the péage machine. There wasn't as much pleasure in driving fast without a passenger, still she raced an articulated lorry onto the toll road. Diane never squealed like Ève and Linette when she drove fast, or went quiet like Jacques, his little grey face watching the cars sail backwards. Diane just carried on talking like nothing was happening.

A Swiss registered Mercedes impatiently flashed his lights behind her. Clotilde yanked the wheel to the right and wagged her finger out of the window as he went by.

The lines of the landscape were flat and angular. Forms that might have broken their shape and taken a stride became nothing more than a cypress planted to protect against wind and sun. Colour seeped onto the planes. The shadows became stripped of possibility, more set in stone, their function decided by the incontrovertible nature of things.

Clotilde didn't see anything mystical in the daybreak, but she noticed suddenly that there was a field of bright yellow sunflowers on her right. In two seconds it was past, replaced by straight rows of vines cutting across the terracotta earth.

The sky, which had been nothing more than a grey ceiling, began to reflect peach and creamy yellow, gradually transforming into fresh blue.

Clotilde yawned then smacked her lips together to generate saliva. She felt an empty waspish sting in her stomach. She reached for the glove box; there was nothing except half a packet of cigarettes and screwed up sweet wrappers. She never ate much, the odd bit of pizza with Diane in front of the cartoons.

After a shift at the Café Rose all she really wanted was a chocolate bar and a glass of wine, and another glass of wine, until she had drunk enough to feel a few years younger. When Diane was in bed she might go out and meet somebody.

The hunger pangs came and went. Clotilde's impatience to get Ève and go home renewed.

She took the exit for the last petrol station before Blagnac airport. Ève was waiting near the green Liquigas stand smoking a stub of a cigarette. Clotilde pulled up to a pump and watched her daughter unobserved. Ève's figure was a line, hardly a hip or a bust to notice. The make-up around her eyes was thick and dark, mimicking some Cleopatra look, but her lips were nude.

She's got to go through it, thought Clotilde. *What can I do about it?*

The nozzle clunked back into the greasy slot.

Clotilde pulled forward into a parking space by the kiosk. Ève looked up. She took a last drag and flicked her cigarette into the gutter.

'How long you been here?' said Clotilde.

'An hour. It doesn't matter.'

'I should think it doesn't, getting me out of bed when it's pitch black.'

Ève handed Clotilde a fifty euro note.

'Here.'

'Where did you get this?'

Ève shrugged and began walking towards the car.

'Want anything? I'm starving,' said Clotilde.

'Coffee, black, lots of sugar.'

Clotilde picked up cigarettes, a four-pack of beer, coffee and croissants.

'Jesus, I feel like I've never eaten. See what happens if you get up too early,' said Clotilde.

'What?'

'You get fat.'

'I smoke too much to get fat,' said Ève.

'You could do with some weight, might fill your clothes better.'

'Huh?'

They pulled back onto the ring road. Clotilde swung into the outside lane.

'Do you have to?'

'I'm overtaking.'

They passed three campervans in convoy.

'So?' said Clotilde.

'What?'

'What happened with Louis, "The Big Night Out?" '

'He's a shit, a grade one shit. I don't want to talk about it, don't ask now. I'll probably tell you when I'm drunk.'

'Ah, then it won't be long until I find out.'

'Whatever you say.'

The traffic was thicker now, cars running excitedly from here to there. It would be lighter once they were away from the high walls and multicoloured rectangles of the blocks of flats on the outskirts of Toulouse.

They didn't sit in silence for long.

'Who's at home?'

'Who'd you think? Linette got up when you called. She made me take the breathalyzer before I set off. You know what she's like. I didn't see Jacques or Diane. You know I'm working. What a fucking start to the day.'

'Yeah,' Ève agreed. 'Can I smoke?'

'Another?'

'It's the coffee.'

Clotilde opened the window a crack. She kept the needle above one hundred and thirty. Ève leaned forward slightly in her seat. Her gaze swept up to the rising horizon as they neared the gorge.

'Will you be busy?'

'It's market day, there's a few tourists, but that doesn't mean anything at the moment. Nobody leaves good tips.'

'You should smile more.'

'Piss-off. You smile all day trying to remember the new menu. It gives me a headache.'

'You're good at it.'

'He's so particular about how you describe things, not just 'salad' but 'garden salad.' I mean, what's the fucking difference?'

'Beats me. By the way, sorry I woke you up.'

'Yeah, well. Don't make a habit of it.'

The Boulanger was quiet and the early-morning dog walkers gone when they arrived back at the flats.

'Don't tell Linette I was easy on you.'

'You weren't.'

'For a four-thirty wake up call!'

'Okay, okay.'

'Carry these.'

'Can I have one?'

'No. Maybe when I get back in the afternoon.'

Clotilde had only been sixteen when Ève was born. Rather than being protective and big-sisterly when Linette, Jacques and Diane arrived, Ève had sided with her mother and tried to escape or avoid the toddler and baby needs of her half-siblings. Being responsible was left to Linette.

'Stay at home today will you, Ève?'

'Why?'

'I'm just asking you.'

They were both slightly out of breath when they reached the third floor landing.

'I'll give up smoking tomorrow,' said Ève, laughing.

'Me too. Come here and kiss me. We're friends again.'

The sound of the television greeted them inside.

'Linette, Jacques, Diane, I'm home!'

There was no reply.

Linette and Jacques were on the sofa in the living room. Diane was sitting on the floor next to a packet of biscuits. Jacques turned around. His face brightened at the sight of his mother and Ève.

'Watcha. We've run out of milk, Mum.'

'I'll bring some back from work.'

'Shit party?' he added, turning to Ève.

'Whatever. Least I'm not sitting here watching shit TV.'

Clotilde reached out and curled a strand of Linette's fair hair around her index finger. Linette moved forward slightly, out of her mother's reach.

'Everyone all right?'

A nerve-jangling advert for kids drinking yoghurt with flying cows and dancing strawberries came on the set.

'I love this one,' Diane squeaked from the floor. She turned around. 'Can we get some, Mum?'

'My God! What happened to your face? It looks like you fell head first off the balcony.'

'It's okay,' Diane replied, raising a hand briefly to her face. 'I got a cold cloth.'

'Something like that doesn't just happen. What did you do?'

Diane fiddled with the unravelling hem of her pyjamas.

'And your arm! Show me.'

Clotilde sidestepped the sofa and knelt by her daughter.

Bruises sometimes hid in the soft brown of her skin, but there was no mistaking this recent impact.

'This wasn't there last night. What have you been up to?'

Clotilde looked more carefully at the scuffed and swollen skin around her daughter's left eye. The blood was still wettish and clotting.

'I was just playing. I slipped.'

'I can't see how…'

'Ssh, Mum. It's come back on,' said Jacques.

'I'm talking with Diane. Where are you going Linette?'

'Where? There's no point being here, I can't hear anything.'

Diane's gaze tracked her sister's movements. She edged closer to her mother, the gentle brown of her eyes taking on a darker hue.

'What's been going on?' said Clotilde.

'Nothing.'

'Jacques?'

'I don't know. They were banging and screaming.'

'Diane? How can you hurt yourself like this? Come on, you're a big girl. Hey, no. Don't start crying, you were fine when I came in. A couple of days and you'll look all right. Now, I have to go out again.'

'I'm going too,' said Ève. 'I had a text. There's a few hours work at the shop.'

'Oh, Diane, your poor face. I suppose it could be worse. Put on a long sleeve top will you? I can't stand to see those marks.'

Diane hesitated.

'Go on. What's wrong?'

Linette stood in the doorway blocking the way.

'You know what she's like. I have to do everything for her,' said Linette.

'I haven't got time for this. Try not to have the telly on all day. Diane, be a good girl. Linette and Jacques will take you to the park later. Come on Ève, let's go.'

'Mum?' peeped Diane.

'Yes.'

'Do I have to stay at home? Can't I come with you?'

'To the café? Don't be silly. All your toys are here, you can watch the cartoons. I'll bring you a slice of tarte au citron if there's any left over.'

'But…'

'Come here and give me a hug. Don't cry. Ssh, you're being silly now. No more accidents while I'm away.'

Diane spoke softly, almost whispering.

'Mum?'

'What?'

'I…please, don't leave me. I want to come. I want to c–'

'You can't. It's work. I'll see you in the afternoon, okay?'

Diane's eyes filled with tears.

There wasn't time to stay any longer. Clotilde manoeuvred Diane onto the sofa then left the room.

It was a bright clear day. Ève lit a cigarette as they walked away from the flats. Clotilde thought about Diane as they passed the playground, she'd been such a happy baby.

Vendor

Of all mornings why this one? Why does she want to come to help?

Madeline reached towards the small cardboard box.

'Are you taking this, Henri?'

'What? Don't, please. I'll take that.'

'No need to be touchy. What's so special anyway?'

'Nothing. I mean, just the new design,' said Henri, slipping it into his pocket.

'It's the necklace, isn't it?'

'Yes, it's in there. I made some alterations, okay?'

'I want to see.'

'We're running late. You'll see when we get there. Come on.'

'Hang on, I'll get something for lunch.'

Madeline walked away from the van towards the château souvenir shop. The tight tubes of her jeans exaggerated her slimness. Even though Henri knew she must be in her fifties from the back she could easily pass for much younger. The style of everything Madeline wore, even the laconic air in which she moved, reminded him more of the teenagers browsing his jewellery stall than the women rummaging though the second hand clothes or browsing the haberdashery stall.

As he waited the sunlight cut across the battlements and behind a stout blockish tower. The place was accustomed to the long hours of heat; centuries in fact.

When Madeline reappeared it was with a bottle of rosé wine swinging jauntily at her hip.

'You didn't lock the door,' said Henri.

'Guillaume will look after things.'

'He's selling tickets.'

'Won't be rushed off his feet. Anyway, Luc can see from the forge. Don't be so sour-faced, we're all making a living.'

She climbed into the van, placing the wine between her feet next to a tiny black leather handbag wrapped round with its strap.

Henri took his keys out of the ignition and stomped back to the door. He had no affection for the château bequeathed to him by his parents, yet he couldn't shake the feeling of responsibility it gave him.

He locked the shop door, a modern paltry thing compared with the ancient timber doors around the courtyard. The irregular shaped room behind was Madeline's domain. It contained fridges with ice creams and cold drinks. There were postcards, wooden swords, guidebooks, plastic knights on horseback, sachets of lavender and mugs printed with cartoon sheep. The plentiful stock left little room for anyone to browse.

Madeline usually sat on a stool outside rather than behind the counter. She occupied herself smoking or chatting to Luc the blacksmith who took cold drinks to refresh himself after stints at the traditional forge where, if the mood to work possessed him, he produced iron roses. These embellished a gate that would eventually replace the plastic sheeting across the steep drop beneath the western window of the chapel.

Luc and Madeline often fell quiet if Henri approached. He would feel his presence was an imposition. Luc would twist one of his heels into the ground; Madeline would stub out her cigarette. Henri would excuse himself, then their conversation would resume.

Occasionally, Henri found it frustrating. But it had not been so recently. He had been too preoccupied to notice their minute comings and goings.

He was in love.

For the first time, the first real time in his life, he was in love. Not just in love but head over heels in love. All his thoughts were devoted to being in love, to the one he loved.

Yes! He *was* in love!

He didn't care if Madeline never sold another pointless trinket, or if Luc set fire to the battlements again, or if Guillaume sold tickets in the nude with a kiosk full of giggling girls.

Nothing else mattered except that he was in love.

What was left of the château could turn to dust – it surely would anyway. The sun was gradually doing the work of demolition, cheered on by the cicadas. Weeds grew in the cracks between the stones. Ash saplings took root in the parched walls just as they did the mountain from which the château had once been constructed.

No, nothing else mattered.

Dust flew up from Henri's feet as he returned to the van. He slammed his door and pushed the van into gear. As he drove out through the mediaeval archway the void for tipping burning embers onto unwanted visitors briefly looked down upon him. It was like an empty eye-socket, clean and perfect. His father had ensured it was meticulously repaired; ten years on and the new stonework still stuck out like a bad patch. Whatever his parents had wanted him to think, Henri had always preferred the neglected parts of the château – he still did.

The curtains on Guillaume's caravan were still drawn. The hut that acted as a ticket kiosk also had its window closed, but it had not been locked up properly. The flap that acted as a counter suspended on two chains hung open. Guillaume's boots sat cock-eyed by the caravan door with half a dozen empty wine bottles.

Henri forced the van into third. The vehicle's nose rocked forward then bucked as the front wheels hit a rut.

'Steady. What's the rush?' said Madeline.

'We're late.'

'Can hardly matter.'

'It does matter,' said Henri. 'I won't get my spot. It annoys the other traders.'

'It annoys the other traders! What a pile of shit. Tell them to get out of the way,' said Madeline.

'I can't tell the–'

'How hard can it be. Say, "This is my spot. Move out of it".'

'It's not…there aren't official spaces.'

'Then what are you whining for?'

'I like to be in the same place,' said Henri.

'That's all?'

'That's all.'

Madeline reached over with her right hand and jerked the gearstick down into second gear. There was a sharp crunching of metal. The van shuddered and slid.

Henri's face twisted. He pulled onto the main road without

even looking for traffic, stones spilling onto the tarmac behind him.

Why did she have to be like this? Why was she even in the van today? Why?

Seemingly unaware of his annoyance Madeline began to fiddle with the radio.

'Anyway,' she said, 'I've been thinking…Shit. I can't get a single thing on this…you should take a leaf from Guillaume's book – and it's a book with many and varied pages if you understand what I mean.'

Henri kept his eyes on the road and his mouth shut. He could feel her looking across at him, her burgundy lips pursed together. He blinked and refocused on the rounds of hay in the fields ahead.

'Yes – very varied, and at times I think illegal, but he says that's all behind him now. But you must have noticed the girls. How they flock to him? He must have something going on. Huh? Something? I mean look as him, that woolly mat on his chest, face like he should be out cutting corn. But he must have something, don't you think?'

Madeline paused to light her cigarette. It was a further irritation to Henri's nerves.

'Don't you think?'

She was waiting for an answer.

What could he say? He couldn't begin to compare the girls, the women that showed up knocking at Guillaume's door with Hélène – the girl *he* loved.

It was as if they were made out of different substances, their flesh composed of different elements that reacted to the most basic things like sunlight differently. Guillaume's women – their skin shone from dried sweat and their eyes had that far focus of someone having recently taken a stimulating substance. Guillaume would pat them absentmindedly on the shoulder or on the knee, nudging fabric aside to rest his hand more comfortably, as if they were a table or chair simply waiting to be rested on; waiting to be used.

Madeline was still watching him.

Henri moved his legs slightly closer together, trying to ease the tension rising between his thighs. How could he confuse

35

them with Hélène.

'I don't know,' he said finally. 'What would I care?'

'Care? You don't need to care, darling. Perhaps you might pick up some tips though. Your mother, I know, never thought of you having a girlfriend, but there's no reason why not is there? Unless you want a boyfriend?'

'Madeline!'

'All I'm saying is,' she bent one knee up and rested it on the dashboard, 'you could have it.' She inhaled, 'A girlfriend. What's wrong with that? What's wrong with me saying that?'

She reached over, this time not for the gearstick; she slapped her hand down on his knee then rocked his leg from side to side. Henri tensed his muscles against her playful jiggle. She had never spoken to him quite like this before. Generally she was only flirtatious if something was awry in the shop – an over order, missing money or stock that she couldn't explain.

He was becoming sure that Madeline had some sort of agenda, some reason for wanting to come with him. He couldn't ever remember her leaving her apartment at the château before nine. *Was it possible that she knew? Or had found out?*

Madeline removed her hand and began to hum a low tune. Henri stared more intently at the road. They passed out of the lines of plane trees to where the valley narrowed and began climbing into the tree-covered slopes.

Henri had not been brought up to run a market stall. His parents had intended he join the family real estate business.

His father had been the 'number one man'. His father was the sort of man you could trust with big decisions. He had bought the château, he had a beautiful wife (aristocratic, it was rumoured) and they had Henri, a cheerful little boy.

But Henri had grown tall, then as the years passed, bulky.

His parents had allowed him to defer his entrance into the business and paid for him to travel. In his own way Henri had seen the world.

It was in Thailand that Henri had learnt to carve. He worked silently for hours, blind to time passing, making small objects that were smooth and satisfying to stroke and hold, little marvels that delighted the hand and eye – the way they rested on the skin was not like an inanimate object at all.

Henri drove on. A cyclist whose rear Madeline watched with unguarded critical interest delayed the van's ascent over the pass. When they eventually overtook she didn't bother to glance at the man's face, she simply blew smoke into the air then said, 'Why d'you still go to the market, Henri?'

'Stock to sell,' he said, trying to sound offhand.

'But you don't *need* to. I bet you're no good at selling anything. You don't *have* to work at all do you?'

'I like it.'

'Really, darling? Really truly?' she said.

He didn't like the direction the conversation was taking. What he most of all wanted to know was why Madeline was coming with him. *Why today?*

It had been a mistake to ask her opinion on the necklace earlier in the week. Straight away she'd signaled over to Luc. He'd abandoned the glowing coals of the forge and a family of Spanish tourists.

'Tie it for me,' she'd said.

'I didn't mean for you to try it,' said Henri.

'I want to see where it hangs. It's important you know. What do you think, Luc?'

'Nice.'

The blacksmith had slipped his hand beneath the carved centrepiece, his knuckle grazing the skin just above the line of Madeline's top.

'Higher,' said Henri. 'It needs to sit higher.'

'I don't think so,' said Madeline.

'Delicate work,' said Luc. 'New design?'

'I've been…well, don't you get bored of making roses?' said Henri.

'No,' replied Luc. 'Looks good on you, Maddy.'

'I'll wear it in the shop,' she'd said, 'an advertisement.'

'No. It's for the stall,' said Henri.

'Pity. You'll get more for it in the shop. Ten euros, twelve if you put it in a box.'

Madeline had patted the ivory coloured shape, traced her finger around the hollow to the tip of the hook.

Henri had untied the necklace; she'd let him take it. He

dropped it gently into a small clear plastic bag and drew his fingers along to seal the top. Luc folded his arms across his leather apron and watched the tourists admiring his roses, waiting for him to return.

'How about a drink, Maddy?'

Henri had left them alone, relieved to have the necklace back in his possession. He went through a door marked, 'Entrée Privée' and written underneath in English, 'Do not open this door'. He laid the package on the kitchen table. Madeline had liked it. *But what did that mean? What kind of woman was she? And, Luc, a blacksmith and an artist of iron roses, had called it delicate. What did that mean?*

Henri had been proud when he'd finished the carving. It was special. It wasn't just a decorative token; it was a symbol of hope. But doubts had crept in. They whitewashed him, hollowed him out, left him wandering aimlessly around the château like when he was a child. That's why he'd shown it to Madeline. He wished he had more confidence.

The van was now descending the sinuous road into the next valley.

If only he could be sure!

He thought he'd seen something in the way Hélène looked at him, something in the way she waited by the stall as the colonie de vacances kids chatted and fidgeted with the bracelets and hairbraids.

'How much?'

'What's this?'

'Do you have it in black? In yellow?'

'It's too small…I don't have change.'

'It's tacky…'

'Lend me some. Where is it?'

As the conversation went round and round all he could think of was Hélène's presence, her nearness.

Henri had decided he would give the necklace to Hélène today. It belonged to her. His heart beat more quickly when he thought about it. *If only Madeline wasn't with him.*

He turned onto the road that went through the gorge.

'Why are you going this way?' said Madeline.

'It makes no difference,' said Henri.

'I thought you were in a hurry.'

He didn't reply. Madeline glanced over to the speedometer.

Craggy limestone formations rose upwards on either side. In some places the cliffs overhung the road and were cut into neat archways to allow two-way traffic.

Henri flicked on his headlights for a short tunnel. When it ended he emerged into a wider forested area that was the beginning of the new valley. Billboards with pictures of kayaks advertised local adventure activities. In the arc of his days this was one of the high-points, this short stretch of road.

Today, no one was waiting to cross at the zebra crossing linking the auberge de jeunesse to the footbridge over the river. He slowed anyway, turning his head and squinting into the shade. It only took an instant to tell if Hélène was there or not. He believed firmly that if she was there, if she was visible at all, he would see her, even if it was just an elbow or a heel, or the swing of the plait that secured her rebellious curly hair.

His heart fled from his body, like a greyhound released from the traps, circling the trees and bushes, around the table-tennis tables, the volley-ball pitch, into the reception area behind the sliding doors and boomeranged back to him. Today there was no one. The kayak sheds were closed. The place was deserted.

'You drive like an old lady, Henri. Come on. I want the toilet.'

Madeline reached between her legs and wriggled the crotch of her jeans.

A couple of minutes later Henri pulled into town. He parked at the end of a line of vans by the railway station and got out quickly. Only the second hand clothes sellers were still turning out their wares. Everyone else was set-up, making the first sales of the morning.

The remaining pitches were around the corner from the main drag of the market. There was no shade and he could already smell the public toilets next to the station and the dog shit on the warming gravel of the boulodrome behind him.

'You could at least help,' he called to Madeline.

'I'm going to catch Clotilde before she gets busy. You can manage.'

She waved a hand over her shoulder.

Henri erected his tables then started to unload his stock. The black cloth was soon heaped with glow-in-the-dark bangles, a type that could be opened and looped together. They were this year's craze and already for sale on three other stalls, but they sold well. He hung up half a dozen fans, pieced together the metal stands for leather thongs with beads and cheap imported pendants of ambiguous significance: skulls, hearts, dolphins…everything had to be taken out of zip-lock plastic bags and displayed.

Lastly, he took out the things he had made, handling them lightly with his already hot fingers. He hurried, although he knew it would be at least an hour before he might see her.

'Where do I sit?'

Madeline's voice startled him.

Without waiting for a reply she pulled down her sunglasses and perched on the low wall of the boulodrome. When a couple of kids from the flats wandered over she lifted her glasses.

'Hands off, Linnette. You too, Jaques. Go on, bugger off.'

The teenagers wandered away. A dark girl skipped after them across the car park.

Henri paused in his unpacking.

'Do you have to be so rude?' he said.

'What? They didn't have any money.' she said.

At about ten-thirty Henri saw the group of a dozen or so children crossing the road. Behind them walked Hélène. Henri's heart pounded like a child overwhelmed by a firework display. *She was here. He loved her and she was here.*

He loved her wide hazel eyes, her dark eyebrows and cupid bow lips. He loved her peachy skin that seemed immune to the sun. He loved her round shoulders, her relaxed athletic limbs. He loved the way she moved like a girl, but had that consciousness of womanhood, of being a leader to the smaller ones.

She was smiling, all the time smiling.

'Good morning, Henri.'

'Hello, Hélène.'

'They all want to spend today.'

He laughed.

'No, no,' she said. 'It's a sad day. They don't want to go home.'

40

'Home?'

'We've already had a few tears. You know they get close so quickly and well, they're all having a great time.'

She shrugged her shoulders.

Henri's mouth was suddenly dry. Home – he hadn't thought of that.

'Going home?' he said.

'Yes. Packing up this morning.' Hélène interrupted herself, 'Marie-Thérèse, I don't think you need that many.'

The girl put back a bracelet then whispered something to her friend.

'Don't worry. I'm keeping an eye on them,' called Madeline from her perch.

Hélène gave a small start.

'Oh. You have help this morning.'

'A friend from the château,' said Henri.

'Château?'

'Home,' he said, 'in the foothills.'

'And the market stall?'

She touched something lightly on the dark cloth.

'For fun,' he said, opening his hands. 'No, that's not what I mean. It's not for fun. It's more…Hélène, I have something for you.'

'For me?'

Henri took the necklace from its bag.

'He's been working on that all week,' called Madeline. She left the wall and sauntered over. 'We wondered who it was for, but he wouldn't tell us. I had to try it on, didn't I?'

Henri's face grew red with indignation.

'Can't you leave me alone!'

'Keep your hair on. You have to show it to her now,' said Madeline.

'Go away!'

'Suit yourself.'

Madeline retreated to her perch.

Hélène had stepped back during their exchange, almost joining the stream of people flowing in and out of the market.

'Please,' said Henri. 'It's true, I did make it for you.'

She looked into his eyes.

All Henri could think was that she was so young, so beautiful; it was so impossible that he could be anything more to her than the man on the market stall. If only she knew how long he'd spent being no one.

'Please, take it.'

He held up the necklace, pinching the ends tightly for fear of letting go. The carving hung between them.

'It must have taken a long time,' she said eventually.

'A going away present,' said Henri. He swallowed hard, holding it a little closer, a little higher.

'Oh? But I'm not going anywhere,' she replied. 'Not until September.'

'Not going?'

'I'm meant to go back to college, but I haven't decided yet. I…it wasn't turning out how I thought.'

'You're staying?'

'Uh-huh.'

Henri lowered the necklace. He stepped closer. He didn't say anything; his lips wouldn't quite work how he wanted them to.

'For God's sake give it to her!' called Madeline from behind the stall. 'Invite the girl out for a drink then bring her back for dinner.'

Neither Henri nor Hélène looked away from each other.

'Well, would you like to?' said Henri.

Hélène smiled.

'I'd love to.'

Bartholomew's Garden

'The day before I left I went with Father Adibe to administer the Sacrament of the Sick. It won't be many days before the man dies.'

While Bartholomew speaks Monica takes a green grape from the plate set between them.

'Is he very old?'

'Monsieur Lenoir? Late seventies, I suppose. It was hard to tell.'

'And why was that?'

'His face was wrapped in bandages apart from one eye. He blinked occasionally to show he understood. Father Adibe was very good with him. Monsieur Lenoir wasn't a regular church goer – not since his wife died.'

'No?'

Bartholomew clears his throat. He leans forward, takes a grape. It bursts inside his mouth, acidic and flowery without being particularly sweet.

Monica and Bartholomew are both aware of the silence in the thick-walled room. The shared awareness is not new.

'It won't be long now,' says Monica glancing at her watch, 'nearly an hour already.'

Bartholomew fidgets with the black cuff of his sleeve. He examines his well-kept fingernails.

'I was thinking, Monica, that so much has happened this past year. I wanted t–'

'Ssh, I think I hear her.'

Bartholomew pauses.

Monica rises from the small table where they have eaten their lunch: Brie – firm and chalky, a farmhouse loaf, mango chutney, tomatoes, and cucumber: an echo of Father Adibe's Pyrenean lunches. Bartholomew had come to enjoy the local hard sheep's cheese; although its ripe smell sometimes resembled vomit, it matched well the salty saucisson sec.

Monica stands by the partly open door, her head tipped to one side. When she is certain it is quiet her shoulders relax. She looks over the polished table.

'Not very much happened while you were away,' says Monica.

'The wall?'

'Oh, that.'

'Terry is coming tomorrow.'

'It was nothing dramatic. A girl practising reverse parking. She was very sorry, couldn't see it in her mirror.' Monica rests a knife on her plate. 'Actually, I think a wider entrance would benefit the church.'

'Perhaps,' replies Bartholomew.

'Tell me more about Sainta Cruixa.'

'You would have liked it,' he says, 'bold colours, baroque styling. ' He smiles at her. 'I suppose it lacked atmosphere – sense of purpose even – being so empty, but the stalwarts keep coming. Father Adibe has become more accepted and...'

'...they need his ministry,' she finishes for him.

It is a common situation.

No one except Monica, her daughter April, a handful of elderly women and a wheelchair-bound man dropped off each morning by his carer, attends his daily mass. The town has a population of nearly thirty thousand.

Other churches fare no better. Peter Simmonds from the Baptist church, a thriving place-to-be church with plastic toddler playthings set out in the hall after service, had admitted to Bartholomew during the annual ecumenical Prayer for Peace afternoon that his numbers are shrinking.

In France there had been more veils, more costume jewellery, but it was the same demographic, the same shades of mahogany hair-dye with creeping inches of grey. Father Adibe moved deliberately slowly presenting the Eucharist to his flock, making eye-contact before placing the white wafer disc on hand or tongue.

Monica comes close to Bartholomew's side.

'Finished?'

He sets a knife on his plate. She places it on a tray on the sideboard. The tray is from Paris. It has a picture of an elegant Chevalier, with a feather plume in his hat, a gold-buttoned jacket and calfskin riding boots. The figure has been given the face of a bad tempered grey cat. Monica likes things like that – she has a sense of humour.

Table clearing progresses no further. Monica pours herself another glass of water and sits back down.

'Did you go anywhere else?'

'A lake,' he replies. 'I swam.'

'You must ha–'

This time there is definitely a sound from upstairs. There are thuds and a high-pitched squeak that turns to a short excited yelp.

Monica sets down her glass and looks at Bartholomew. Like the grapes her eyes are sharp and green. They reflect the glow of the laburnum leaves around the low window. It is in moments like these that Bartholomew feels courage.

Monica stays still for a moment then she stands up and walks to the doorway.

'April will be excited to see you.'

'It feels like I've been back for days already,' Bartholomew replies.

He listens and waits.

When she arrives April *is* excited.

Monica carries her into the room. April's red hair, ruffled after her sleep, sticks out at odd angles. Bartholomew notices the sun has lightened it since he has been away; temperatures have been as high in England as in France.

Monica kisses her daughter on the temple and smooths down a cluster of rogue hairs. They sit together.

'Hello, April. How are you today?' says Bartholomew.

April reaches forward with two hands, opening and closing her fingers, grabbing the air to drag Bartholomew closer.

'I know,' he says. 'I have something for you.'

Monica looks over to him, a short defiant stare.

'It's something small,' he says.

From his trouser pocket he pulls out a small wooden case. It is carved rather like the shape of a walnut shell and has a tiny metal hinge. He passes it to Monica.

April takes it from her mother. She shakes it up and down.

'Open it,' he says.

Monica retrieves the gift and obeys. She smiles.

'Look inside, April. See!'

Inside the case is a tiny brightly painted beetle whose legs scurry to and fro as the box wobbles.

April laughs, grabs the box, closes the lid and shakes it again.

Her cheeks are fatter and wider compared with most four year olds; her eyelids are heavier; her chin broader. Her lips habitually form an 'O' shape when she tries to speak. Monica has taught her sign language to express some needs. This includes wanting the toilet, a sign April now makes.

'She seems happy,' he says.

'She's always happy,' says Monica.

Bartholomew rises from his chair.

'I'll tidy up. Then I must go.'

Monica and April leave the room. As Bartholomew clears the table he thinks about Monsieur Lenoir; the way his eye had followed Father Adibe's hand as he made the final blessing; the blinking rheumy eye.

The table is cleared well before there are any signs of Monica and April finishing in the bathroom upstairs.

Bartholomew waits in the hallway. The uneven surface of the walls moulds the soft light into vertical white landscapes. He stares into the pottery bowl where Monica keeps her house and car keys. Eventually there is a flush, the sound of running water. There is a creak as Monica places her foot on the first step. She has seen Bartholomew waiting, but now he pretends to hurry.

'I'll see you tomorrow morning,' he says.

'Where are you this afternoon?'

'Brother James is at the presbytery until tomorrow. I have to go.'

He points to the front door.

Monica strokes the little girl's hair. Bartholomew and Monica's gaze meets for a moment. Then he leaves.

Bartholomew strolls past the gardens of the neighbouring cottages, they are enclosed by iron railings sunk into a low wall. The cottages lean together forming one side of an alleyway paved with irregular flat stones. He thinks about his congregation, their watching and knowing. It can be hard to bear.

Soon he is between high red brick walls then emerges at the

telephone box by the old cobblers. It is now a hair salon. Opposite is the old greengrocers – now a funeral parlour. It is a short walk along the main road to the church.

Bartholomew's temporary replacement, Brother James Laurie, concelebrates mass the next morning. Afterwards they take lunch together in the presbytery: bread rolls, quiche and coleslaw all from the supermarket. Brother James extols the spacious accommodation and admonishes Bartholomew for the state of the garden. Brother James has a gap between his front two teeth, a bald spot and silver rimmed spectacles. He looks like a monk.

'Lady's Mantle will take over if you let it. It's very invasive.'

'It certainly thrives.'

'Pull it all up if I were you. Try something slower growing. I'm coming around to planting more bulbs. Nerines are pretty, barely any work to them.'

'I'll have a think about it. The garden needs more attention than I give it,' says Bartholomew.

Brother James's fork hovers over the last slice of quiche.

'Do you mind?'

Bartholomew shakes his head. He takes a sip of water; unconsciously he drums his fingers while watching Brother James eat. When he has finished Bartholomew clears the table.

'One of the parishioners,' begins Brother James, 'the mother with the Down's girl, she seemed to know plenty about plants. You could ask her for advice.'

'Who?'

'The woman with the Down's girl. She came to mass today. They both did.'

'Yes, yes. I should do something.'

'Lucky to still have the space, especially with the school expanding.'

Bartholomew nods. He is ready for Brother James to leave.

There is not long to wait. After lunch the suitcases are moved from the hallway to the car. Bartholomew and Brother James shake hands and agree that the arrangement works well. Bartholomew closes the door and listens to the car merge with the stream of traffic. He slips two fingers between the stiff fabric collar and his throat. What was it Brother James said?

47

'The woman with green eyes and the Down's girl.'

He hears the scrape-tumble of a cement mixer. It reminds him about the car park wall. Bartholomew re-opens the front door and goes back outside.

Terry the builder thrusts a bucket towards the orange mixer, jerking it to a stop before it hits the rotating drum. Water sloshes out. On the ground a piece of plywood supports a pile of sand. Several bags of cement are nearby. There is a neat stack of bricks ready for re-use, the old mortar already chipped off.

'How's progress?' says Bartholomew.

Terry looks up from the mixer then wipes an arm across his forehead.

'Getting there,' he says.

Bartholomew looks at the stump where the old wall terminated.

'Can you flatten it out?'

'Could do.'

The builder is bare-chested. He has a neat, slim torso. Rising over the edge of his low-slung jeans Bartholomew can see the elastic of Terry's underwear. The word 'Guess' is embroidered in white on a background of dark blue. Terry's hair is shaved except for an inch wide strip running from the top of his forehead to the base of his neck. The hair is short, erect and dyed bright vermillion.

Bartholomew takes a few paces backwards until he stands level with the entrance to the Lady Chapel. The laurel hedge separating the church from the street is over eight feet high. It obscures the church windows from pedestrians and vice versa. It also makes pulling out onto the road awkward.

On the intact side of the entrance there is a small square pillar with a stone pyramid balanced on top. A matching pyramid lies near to the pile of sand.

'A wider entrance might be more practical,' says Bartholomew.

'It's up to you,' says Terry. 'It's not an insurance job is it?'

Terry also has a pierced nose. The stud catches the light.

Bartholomew wonders who dyes Terry's brightly coloured strip of hair. Who is responsible for the up-keep of this hairstyle? He imagines two men in a white bathroom, a neat line of tools and ointments laid out on a cabinet.

'No. I want it put back the way it was.'

Terry nods.

Bartholomew stays and watches the mortar tipped out. Terry uses a trowel to scoop a portion onto a small flat board then flips and flops it this way and that until an even mound is formed. He fills the trowel and deftly wipes and shapes the mortar onto the surface of a reclaimed brick.

Bartholomew's attention drifts to the wooden door of the church. That morning Monica had withdrawn with April into the Lady Chapel during the responsorial psalm. It wasn't soundproof, but the squeaks and squeals were quieter.

She'd held April on her hip as she received communion on her tongue. April had pulled at her mother's t-shirt and stared at Bartholomew while Monica lowered her eyes and said, 'Amen.' He'd thought Monica looked more serious than usual.

The glare of the sun reflects off every surface of the car park. *My spirit is weak*, thinks Bartholomew.

'Terry, I've changed my mind. Make it wider.'

'Wider?'

'Yes. Both sides. Take a good three feet off. Don't worry about putting those tops back on either. They'll only get knocked off.'

Father Bartholomew crosses back to the presbytery. He steps over a dandelion blooming between the flag stones, twists sideways to get past an ill-disciplined climbing rose.

Upstairs, he unzips his holiday case and takes out the clothes he had worn at the lake – still gritty, carrying scent different to the second-hand shop odour that lingers in the presbytery.

In the shed where parish volunteers keep the lawnmower he finds a hand trowel, a pair of secateurs and a cracked bucket.

Bartholomew becomes engrossed in his work, avoiding thorns, clipping away old blooms and new growth. The sound of building and traffic fades.

'Shall I put them in water?'

'What? Sorry, Monica. I'm pruning.'

'I can see,' she says.

'Do you think it needs it?'

'It's needed it for years,' she says.

'Hello, April,' he says.

'Can she dig there?'

'Of course,' he smiles. 'It doesn't matter.'

Bartholomew points at the Lady's Mantle.

'Brother James said I should…actually never mind.' He pauses then closes the secateurs. 'Monica, I've decided. I'm going to speak to Bishop Neville.'

'About me?'

'It's human, heartfelt, faulted…real. The one thing it's not is a failure of faith.'

Monica looks at the cuttings around her feet.

'Do you think we can possibly be good people?'

'What do you mean?'

'I can't encourage you,' she says.

Then Bartholomew recalls something.

'Remember the man in France I ministered to?'

'Monsieur Lenoir?'

'Yes. Father Adibe told me that before he turned the gun on himself Monsieur Lenoir had shot at a young man – out of passion. They'd all watched him, seen his behaviour change. No one thought the old man would ever do anything. The *real* scandal was that he *acted*. Do you know there's a movement in Nigeria for married priests?'

For a moment there is silence.

'He'll interrogate you.'

'Bishop Neville? I know.'

'I love my church, Bartholomew.'

'It's not restlessness. It's not dissatisfaction with the church…'

'Bartholomew.'

'Yes.'

'I don't doubt you.'

'Thank you,' he says.

Monica crouches down next to April. She picks up a couple of cuttings and puts them in the bucket.

'The rose will grow back strongly,' she says, 'if properly pruned. The Lady's Mantle will have seeded everywhere. It's a plant that roams.'

'Yes,' says Bartholomew, 'I know.'

Cumulonimbus

Jeanie is listening to her mother with her eyes half closed.

'They only stock up once a season, so by the time we were here they had run out of Maxibon. We couldn't come any earlier, not last year.'

Her mother is working a foot pump, she is wearing a printed kaftan over a black one-piece. Mrs Franklin, whose face is the colour of a walnut, is patiently pinching the transparent valve of the blowup dinghy. Satisfied that the sides are firm, the valve is plugged.

'Could you pass the sun cream, Jackie?' says Jeanie's mother. 'Factor thirty for my two I'm afraid – not everybody has your skin. Come here, Sophia. Hold your hair up.'

Jeanie's sister Sophia half-heartedly makes a shelf with her arms to lift the fair hair from her shoulders.

'You're lucky, Jackie. Arthur's so dark I doubt you'll need to put anything on him at all after a couple of days.'

'I can do it, Mum,' says Sophia.

'You'll need to do your stomach, since you're determined to wear that bikini. What do you think, Jackie? It's her first year wearing one. I suppose she'll fill it soon enough. Come on, Jeanie. You too. Don't fuss.'

Jeanie is older by nearly two years. She is wearing a modestly cut bright green swimsuit.

'I want some chips,' says Sophia.

'For goodness sake. Can't you sit for a while or have a swim? I've just spent twenty minutes inflating this boat.'

'I'll take the boat out,' says Jeanie, taking hold of the short nylon rope.

'I'll come,' says Sophia. 'Get some chips though, Mum.'

'No. You wait until you get back.'

The sisters carry the dinghy between them and wade into the lake.

When the girls are out of earshot Jeanie says, 'It's too hot for chips. Ask for ice cream.'

'She's just in a bad mood,' says Sophia.

The water pinches at Jeanie's thighs distracting her from further conversation. She glances over at the turquoise sun umbrellas and plastic chairs and tables. The kiosk is open, one window selling drinks and ices, the other *frites* and light meals.

'I'm going to climb on,' says Sophia.

Jeanie wraps the nylon cord around her hand and steadies the boat. It would hold two smaller children, but the sisters are no longer small.

The bottom of the artificial lake turns from sand to gritty silt. Fronds of weeds slide between Jeanie's toes, brushing her shins and calves. Jeanie dips a hand into the water then sloshes her arms and tummy. The rippling water wets the underside of her swimsuit. She shivers then bends her legs to bring the surface up to her ribs.

The umbrellas catch her attention again. Jeanie recalls a scene from last summer; she remembers her mother's clipped censorious tones.

'Really, they should put some clothes on. This is a café. *Some people are having meals.* They're only little I know, and it is hot, but I'm sure it can't be too much trouble to get something on them.' Her mother had sighed discontentedly, then said, 'Sophia, don't lick it like that. Can't you do *anything* without making a mess?'

A few minutes later, Sophia's ice-lolly was teetering on the brink of splitting and falling. Jeanie had been watching the toddler happily banging the table with her free hand and licking a neon-green lolly of her own, when under the slatted seat a few drops then a steady dribble of urine rained down onto the dusty grass. No one took any notice except Jeanie's mother.

'Wouldn't have taken a moment to put a nappy on. We'll have to watch where we sit from now on. It's certainly not hygienic. Mind you, she can't be twenty can she?' She'd sipped her ice-tea then added, 'You can have one more swim, then I want to head back to the house. It'll be too hot for anything this afternoon.'

While Sophia suffered her hands to be wiped, Jeanie had watched the young woman. She was wearing middle-eastern style trousers, pleated and flowing over her hips and gathered around her ankles. Her skin was smooth and rounded, a shade or two darker than the plump leg of the baby that gripped the saddle of her hip. Jeanie noticed how the woman's bandeau bikini top tucked under her breasts, rising in a gentle curve across her cleavage. The woman absentmindedly pecked the baby's forehead with a kiss. Without the need for words the toddler squirmed out of her chair and took the young mother's outstretched hand.

Jeanie had rather liked the way the young woman held the baby, skin-to-skin, and the dark slit of the toddler's tiny bottom wiggling over the grass. She had wondered if they would see them again this year.

Sophia begins kicking her legs to propel the boat. Jeanie defends herself against the splashes.

'Stop! I don't want to get my hair wet.'

'God, you're so boring. You just don't want to get out of your depth.'

Jeanie lets go of the rope and shoves the dinghy towards the buoys marking the swimming area. The boat rocks, water sloshes inside.

'Everyone's so boring!' shouts Sophia, as she kicks and floats away.

Jeanie turns to the shore. It isn't long before she can pick out the funny black and gold overshirt her mother had taken to covering herself with. She's standing with one hand raised to shield her eyes from the glare. Jeanie can see the supine tawny body of Mrs Franklin on a towel. Nearby, Arthur is tipping sand out of a bucket.

On impulse Jeanie arches her back and half flips, half falls backwards, skimming beneath the water with her eyes shut tight. She twists then swims in slow even strokes towards Sophia.

'Budge up.'

Sophia shifts sideways. Both girls lie side by side, tummies pressing into the base of the dinghy, arms folded, legs dangling into the water. The sides deform into a shallow 'v' allowing water to lap in and out of the boat.

The dinghy rotates slowly until it faces away from the artificial beach and blue umbrellas, towards the far shore. Orange tent domes can be seen through the trees. There is cool, dark green shade at the water's edge. 'Someone could be watching us from the bank,' says Sophia. 'You know 'cos they're a pervert.' She pauses. 'Why did you let mum buy you that swimsuit?'

'She says it suits me.'

'Green? It's…I don't know.'

'What does it matter?' says Jeanie. 'I don't know anyone here.'

Sophia lifts her chin. She looks for a moment at the warning triangle printed on the inflated plastic – in half a dozen languages it says that on no account should the item be used as a boat – then she says, 'D'you know I tried smoking at Clare Hall's party. Craig was there, even though he's meant to be grounded. And Shaun Stevens gave me two bottles of Bacardi Breezer.'

'What's Shaun like?'

'Don't know really,' says Sophia.

'No?'

'He wanted to get off with me.'

Sophia closes her eyes and lets her head sink into the warm plastic membrane. The heat is releasing a strong smell of vinyl.

'He tried to put his hand up my shirt,' she says, her eyes still closed. 'I told him not to bother. God, I hope they get bigger soon.'

Jeanie taps her fingers on the water and hums the tune of 'Happy Birthday' as they float.

'It needs more air,' says Sophia.

'Huh?'

'It's going soft.'

Jeanie reaches out a hand and pushes away from the rope.

'Y'know green really doesn't suit you,' says Sophia. 'Leave it somewhere. Make her buy you a bikini. At least it would fit you.'

They kick back to shore. Soon, they come level with a toddler pointing to something in the water.

'Poisson! Poisson!'

Jeanie sees the finger length light-green fish schooling together in areas of undisturbed water. They have brownish patches on their bodies and blunt faces with flat black eyes.

A fleeting fantasy passes through her mind, of the fish arranged like stars around her feet, nibbling her flesh. The toddler lurches forward, both hands outstretched. The fish scatter.

Jeanie eases herself out of the boat and walks onto the sand. Her mother is still talking; Mrs Franklin is not replying, she is quite possibly asleep.

'...but, it's not about the money...don't worry it's not a fight breaking out, all that noise. I think the man must be disabled. They've been sensible taking a place in the shade. It won't be long until the sand is unbearable.'

'Can I have some euros?' asks Jeanie.

'What for?'

'I want a drink. Can I get anything for you Mrs Fra– I mean Jackie?'

'No, darling. Arthur might come with you though. There's money in my sunglasses case if he wants anything.'

Arthur looks up from the sloppy puddle he has been enlarging. Jeanie takes his gritty hand in hers.

'Actually, I might get myself something,' says Jeanie's mother.

'I'll get it for you,' says Jeanie.

'No. I'll come and see what they have.'

Arthur's hand rests placidly in Jeanie's as they walk along. As they pass the toilet block a man enters the Gents. He is bare-chested, wearing a white flat cap and tailored shorts. The urinals are obscured by a low wall, but from the waist up the man remains visible. Jeanie notices how his shoulders flex and his neck extends as he urinates. It gives her a funny feeling.

'Do you need the toilet, Arthur?' says Jeanie's mother. 'I've brought toilet paper.'

Arthur shakes his head, keeping his gaze fixed in the direction of the blue umbrellas.

They come to a stop at the ice cream menu.

'I should think they have everything. You can choose whatever you like, Arthur. Really, they are expensive, but there's nowhere else.'

Arthur points.

'That one? It's very big. Are you sure? Put Mrs Franklin's money away, Jeanie. I'll pay for it. Anything else? What about one of those for Sophia?'

'She wants chips. I'm getting a coke.'

'*Not* very refreshing, Jeanie.'

Jeanie leaves her mother and walks with Arthur to the right hand window. There are balls, inflatables and sets of sand toys for sale behind the counter but no sign of anyone serving. Jeanie moves on to the next window.

'This is where they do chips, Arthur,' she says. 'You can have mayonnaise, ketchup or mustard. You press here and it squirts out.'

A man wearing a white apron and T-shirt steps away from the fryer. A lick of dark hair escapes from beneath his catering hat.

'Bonjour.'

'Frites, s'il vous plait,' says Jeanie. 'Un coke aussi.'

Jeanie feels a tap on her shoulder. It's her mother.

'You're in the wrong place, Jeanie. We're buying ice-creams.'

She gestures for Jeanie to move.

'Pas de problem,' says the man.

Jeanie's mother draws breath then makes her order.

'The stripy one, that's it. Oh, I don't know. I'll have one of those. And we'll get a lemon one as well.'

'I've ordered chips,' says Jeanie.

'Really? Well if you–'

The man places the ice creams on the counter and passes Jeanie her coke. The condensation is missing where he has touched the can. The smooth wet metal buckles slightly beneath her fingers.

Jeanie's mother peers inside her purse rolling the coins from side to side.

'How much? I mean, c'est combien?'

'Neuf et cinquante.'

The man behind the counter turns his head towards Jeanie. He gives her a conspiratorial smile then looks sideways back to her mother.

Arthur pumps on the mayonnaise. The plastic tray is so hot

Jeanie has to change hands while walking along back to the sand.

Sophia only pecks at the chips, as if she can be barely bothered to eat. In contrast, Jeanie suddenly feels hungry. She takes the tray and eats chip after chip until they're all gone.

Afterwards, looking out on the lake and leaning back on her elbows to let her swimsuit dry, Jeanie remembers something else that happened the year before; something she made the mistake of telling her mother about.

It had been around four-thirty during a hot afternoon. Everyone else had retreated inside. She had been writing postcards, lying on a pool lounger in the shade. From her position she could see the shutters of the upper floor of a house in the next street. They had opened and a man, tanned, broad-chested – she couldn't tell if he were young or old – had stood in the open window. A sheet was wound around his waist. He had leaned on the windowsill for a moment looking down on her. Then he had left the window. It had been quite easy to see into the room behind where he stood. It must have had a skylight or something to make the room so light. She could see the edge of a bed with black iron ends and white sheets. The room had white walls. She saw the man sit down on the edge of the bed. She saw from his movements that he was unfolding the sheet from around his waist. And she had stayed exactly where she was.

Secret

Théo sat naked on the bed. He was so lost in thought that for several seconds it didn't register that somewhere below a woman's voice called his name.

'I'm awake, Mama,' he called over his shoulder.

He gathered the sheet around his thighs, looked once more at the girl on the sun lounger in the courtyard of the old solicitor's house then rose to his feet.

It was a short distance to his private bathroom. In here it was even warmer than the bedroom. The single window had long been painted shut and the volet was permanently closed, admitting only a dozen or so slivers of horizontal light at certain times of the day.

There was a sink, whose hot tap was easily unseated from its mounting. Théo had abandoned using it after clumsily causing a flood the winter he broke his collarbone. After the accident, his mother had restricted him to cycling in the town, forbidding the mountain tracks. When Théo outgrew his bicycle he was not provided with another.

There was a toilet, with a blackened wooden seat and porcelain bowl that had old-fashioned angular sides – so much less sinuous than the modern facilities installed in the pharmacy where he worked.

There was also a bidet, the only item in the room to have suffered any replacement of its original parts. The glinting three-way silver fitting was the most eye-catching thing in the room until Théo's finger flicked a narrow switch and the dull bulb in the lamp overhanging the mirror came to life. This procedure was something he often neglected, so familiar were the shadows in the enclosed room. They varied little day or night because of the two tall lamps on the bridge by the front of the house.

If he wanted to, Théo could lean out from the vantage point of his bedroom window and see a slice of the activity in the square across the river. Today he stayed away from the window. He dressed for the afternoon at work then descended through the layers of the house.

'You were asleep a long time,' said his mother.

'It's hot.'

'Drink something before you go.'

She was running cold water over a sieve filled with green lentils. A basket of vegetables from the allotment sat on the scrubbed kitchen table.

'They have air-conditioning,' he said.

'Psh. It'll make you ill.'

'Not so far,' he replied. He bent and kissed her on the temple. 'I'll see you this evening.'

'Don't be late. It's enough tha–'

'I won't be late, Mama.'

Théo left her; her hand swirling like a fortune teller's.

Compared to the boxy kitchen the narrow street felt airy and open. It was an illusion he knew, but still he welcomed the temporary sensation.

A boy with a sagging plastic bag of groceries skiffled past, deliberately scraping the toe of his sandal. A customer, an old man from what had jokingly started to be called the 'North African Quarter,' lifted his stick in greeting as Théo went past.

Théo thought back to the girl on the sun lounger, to the damp shadow around where her swimsuit had rested. He had hoped that he would resist, that he would not dwell on the detail. He didn't want to.

Summer and its afternoon sleeps, which were inexcusable at any other time of the year, had always been Théo's favourite season. Sounds and smells travelled across borders that usually held them in check; life was rich. His mother was reminded of her native Spain and could be more forgiving.

They rarely saw his father during the summer – not that his presence was an irritation in any way – there was paid gardening and work to be done in the allotment. When Théo was younger, he'd enjoyed sitting in the shade of the tumbledown allotment shed, an oil-cloth pulled over the work table. Sometimes company had gathered. Life had been sociable.

Now Théo had lost touch with most of his generation, a fact

his mother found strange because he had been a popular boy. She quizzed him about it repeatedly.

'What about Jérôme?'

'He's too busy to spend time over here.'

'Guillaume? Charles? You all used to be inseparable.'

'They have their own lives, Mama.'

'I just don't understand it. What about the girls? You're such a handsome man.'

'Mama, please. I'm not lonely.'

'Of course you're not lonely. I just don't understand it.'

The last time they had had the conversation she'd been preparing broad beans, tumbling them into the colander by sliding her thumb along the velvet cases. Plink-plink-plink.

There was Geneviève. He still met her for lunch on Fridays at Café Rose. The habit had begun soon after she returned from accountancy training and had been settling back to being in town. Since then she had married, had two children and until recently worked at the local tax office. If she had suggested they meet up now for the first time he would more than likely have refused out of politeness. Her life had moved on.

Sometimes Geneviève would talk about her children.

'Sebastien pinches Nico when he thinks I'm not looking. It drives me wild – Nico never cries out, sits there with tears in his eyes. What can I do?'

'I'm sure he will grow out of it,' Théo would reply.

It was his policy never to offer advice.

Sometimes she would talk about her husband.

'…and he said Lyon was the only place they speak French properly. Théo, can you believe it? I wonder sometimes.'

At the end of lunch Théo would slide money across the table. Geneviève would ignore it or say, 'Please, put that away. I'm sure it's my turn to pay. What did we have? Really, is it that much? Well it makes no difference to me.'

Last week she had been waiting for him at a table on the far side of the terrace.

'Théo! Théo! Over here. Do you think the food will be better with the new chef? I must smoke, but you don't mind do you? It's really been too much today. That office! Those people! I can't believe I used to be in the thick of it. They still call me up for advice. There's one man, I'm sure you know who I'm talking about, claiming reimbursement for his dog's veterinary bills. His justification? He's required to be in good mental and physical health for his job and the dog – get this – is providing an exercise service. I don't know if his wife is claiming the same thing but I wouldn't be surprised. Common sense went out of the window long ago in this field. I think he might get away with it.'

'He'll grow out of it,' said Théo.

'Pardon?'

'I mean, you're right. It's ridiculous.'

Geneviève had looked at him more closely.

'What's distracting you?'

'Nothing…something I saw, I suppose.'

The waitress arrived. Clotilde told them the specials and took their order without any hint of interest in their conversation even though they were familiar customers.

'Do you know the cat woman?' said Théo, when she had gone.

'Madam Crébor?'

Théo leaned forward slightly in his chair.

'I think she's turning into a cat – see her hair, her face. Next time you walk past take a better look.'

'Théo, you're terrible,' Geneviève laughed.

'It's not just the whiskers. I'm sure I saw her pouring Pastis into a saucer.'

Geneviève laughed again. She'd leaned back and tapped ash over the stone wall where the steep banks dropped down to the river.

If Théo ever expressed any doubt in the value of his companionship Geneviève would admonish him, saying that seeing him was essential.

'At least there's no bullshit with you,' she'd said once.

Sometimes when he returned to the shop after one of these lunches he'd feel disoriented. The shelving would seem high, he'd be suddenly conscious of the flesh-coloured bandages, the boxes of suppositories, the feminine products, the condoms, the advice leaflets…

He'd fold up his jacket then pause, holding onto the still

warm fabric for a few seconds to get his bearings before sitting at his desk. Then he'd funnel all his concentration into parceling up photographs ready for collection.

This morning he'd been looking forward to lunch with Geneviève more than ordinarily. The cuisine at Café Rose had improved with the arrival of the chef Jean, so far without any increase in price. Théo had yet to sample the fillet of veal – something his mother never cooked.

He slotted envelopes into their alphabetical position, his back to the entrance of the shop. Some packages he held for longer than others, sometimes rubbing his thumb over the plastic window where the corner of certain photographs peeked through, unconsciously reluctant to file them away.

'Théo? Hey, Théo.'

He had looked up, startled.

'What? Sorry I was just…Geneviève? What can I do for you?'

'Nothing. I came to say lunch is off. Nico's hurt his wrist at school. I have to take him to the hospital.'

'Of course,' he said. 'Another time.'

'Sorry, Théo. Maybe this evening. I'd like a drink. We never go out in the evening.'

She was talking even more quickly than usual. Her cheeks were flushed.

'Are you sure? Won't you have to stay at home?' said Théo.

'Why should I? Are you busy?' she said, impatiently.

'No.'

'Okay then. Give me some of that bandage. No, the other. That's it. Ten o'clock at the café. I'll see you.'

She paid then hurried out of the shop without making further conversation.

The remainder of the morning dragged. When twelve o'clock arrived Théo had told the pharmacist that he would be back at four to process the rest of the days orders. As he stepped out into the street he glanced back. The red digital numbers in the shop window showed a temperature of thirty-seven degrees.

A high white line separated the tenements either side of the narrow street, gap-toothed patterns of shade delineating one neighbour from the next.

His mother had prepared tomatoes and beans, served with slices of spicy sausage. They ate without exchanging many words. Her face was flat, pulled down by the weight of one of her sudden moods of homesickness.

'I'm going to rest,' he told her.

'If you can,' she said, 'in this place…with these people, wha–'

'Mama, please. It's hot.'

She looked across at him sharply.

'Psh. Calling this hot?'

'Thank you for lunch.'

'Leave everything. You know I don't expect you to do that. Go, go and rest.'

Nearly two hours had gone past while Théo slept. And while he slept, yellow ants explored the dry cracks in the bathroom nibbling morsels of soap and skin before retreating back through the tiles.

When Théo awoke he'd stretched then lay for a moment stroking the hairs growing out of a mole on his jaw. He'd stared at the ceiling. A small bright dot the size of a coin with medusoid tails darted here and there around the inside of the room. He'd swung his legs around and looked out of the window to find its source.

It was then he'd spotted the girl on the lounger. As she wrote the bright flash of her metal pen was reflecting into his room.

That afternoon at work he thought about her again. As he slid closed the drawers of photographs – some long since forgotten by their owners, others still smelling faintly of vinegar – he imagined that she had yellow eyes like a cat's. Immediately, he also thought of Madame Crébor. He had a strange vision of the old woman, her face crudely painted with face make-up; with orange and white cheeks and thick black whiskers; she was hissing, hands bent-wristed in an imitation of cats' paws.

He tried to shake the image and return to the memory of the girl by the blue pool with her postcards and glass of lemonade. Still the vision of the cat woman persisted.

Later, as Théo walked back to his parents' house through the dark streets it returned more forcibly, seeming to lurk in the shadows.

His gaze sought lit windows for distraction. There was no

relief in the sordid little kitchens with their melamine tables and cupboards studded with half-moon handles – like half open mouths waiting to bite the fingers of anyone foolish enough to insert them.

A pair of teenagers zipped past him on motorbikes, gesturing obscenely with their hands. Decline and decay in all its various stages were on display for the few who passed down the street. Théo found it hard to imagine that the old centre of town had ever been anything less than squalid, even though he knew it had once prospered; his father, like many others had lost his employment when the factory closed.

At least his parents' were by the river; the air channeling over the water brought some respite to the stifling nights.

The smell of onions greeted Théo when he entered the house. His father was in the narrow hall, sliding his feet into a pair of grimy indoor flip-flops.

'Eat,' he said to Théo. 'Come on.'

Théo deposited his jacket.

'I mustn't have too much,' said Théo once seated. 'Less than that please, Mama. I'm seeing Geneviève at the café.'

'You don't want to eat it. Is that what you say?'

'No, Mama. I don't need so much. Look at me.'

'What about winter? Your father spends all da–'

'What…eh? Don't bring me into it.'

His father held his knife and fork vertical, resting his wrists on the table; wrists and arms of old muscle built from repeating the same movements over and over again.

Théo slid his fork under the discs of lentils and began to eat methodically. His mother took only a quick glance at her own plate so intently did she watch her son.

After dinner they retired to the lowest room of the house, the one with a balcony and steps leading down to a scrubby piece of ground that flooded in the winter. His mother sat with her sewing basket slowly unpicking a patch, his father held a newspaper. The television was on, with the volume turned down very low so it was possible to hear the rush of the river and the cries of birds arguing in their roosts.

It was usual for Théo to sit before the television, taking the newspaper when his father was finished.

The scene, so static over days and years, held a strange magic. Part of Théo believed it could never have been otherwise.

There was another truth though. For other things had happened. And they had also happened again and again, as if they had always been so and always would be so.

After an interval he hoped his mother would find decent Théo left his parents sitting together. He returned through the food-scented kitchen without reaching for the light, turned the sharp corner to the stairs then ascended. His head came level with the floorboards and for a moment he saw through the banister into his parents' room, underneath the bed where a fuzz of dust dared to lie. Lit as it was now, by the fading sky over the mountains and from the lamps on the bridge, he was transported back to that other earlier truth.

His mother was lying on the bed fully clothed, moving restlessly and speaking, saying something in Spanish. His father stood next to her. His head bowed, his hands held together almost like the priest after communion when the congregation was silent.

Théo knew some Spanish words, but didn't understand everything his mother said. He'd stayed there watching. She had become more and more agitated until she sat up on the bed, pointing at his father. She held her belly then began weeping, scratching at her clothes, pulling them apart so much so that his father took some of the bedclothes and started to wrap them around her.

'Antonia, stop. Stop!'

'You cannot love me. You cannot!'

She loosened her hair, letting it flow over her shoulders.

'Look at me. Look at me now. Eh?'

His father became still for a moment then reached across and closed the bedroom door.

Théo had stayed where he was on the stairs in the near darkness, not daring to move until everything was quiet.

But it wasn't this incident, or pattern of incidents that disturbed him most. His parents were grown-ups. What importance was it to him what they did?

It was a singular event later on, when his mother had taken Théo aside to speak to him. There had been no special occasion in his mind. No reason. He had been twelve.

'Théo, come here. I'll take that.'

She lifted the basket of apricots from his arms.

'Sit. Sit. So, we are the same height now. Eh?' she observed. 'There is something I need to tell you, Théo.'

Théo had glanced through to the back room window. He'd been going to meet Guillaume at a new spot to fish for trout when his mother had called him back. He felt bad about keeping his friend waiting.

She didn't say anything at first, just scrutinized him, like some piece of food left on his plate. She was calm – he remembered she had been in a level-headed mood all day. Piles of fruit waited in preparation for jam making on the table.

'A woman will always know,' she said, without any further introduction. 'However clever you think you are. However hard you scrub. She will know. You will not be able to hide what you've done. And you will never, *never* satisfy her afterwards. You will be a weak man…'

She pointed a finger at his groin.

'…your seed will be weak…'

Her finger came closer, piercing the air in the kitchen as if it were a membrane.

'…always.'

Théo stared at the finger, mesmerized even though it was now stationary between them.

A light wind blew up from the water, ruffling his mother's dark hair, moving the fabric of his T-shirt against his chest. Blood rushed to his cheeks.

He couldn't be certain how much time passed before he spoke.

'Can I go?'

'Yes,' she said.

She picked up her paring knife.

Not long afterwards, his mother began to take a regular prescription from the pharmacist; the confrontations, the arguments with his father that had seemed to drag on and on into the night, gradually ceased.

This evening as Théo climbed the stairs it had all come back to him.

When he reached his bedroom he stood in front of the mirror, face flushed. It felt fine that he was going to the café, going to see some life for once. It was fine to be going to see Geneviève.

He laid a fresh shirt on his bed then stole down to the second floor, through the unused second bedroom to the shower room. He had been dwelling again on the teenage girl. He wished he hadn't. He wished he didn't need to. His hands moved under the running water.

By the time he was ready to leave the house it was quarter to ten. He assumed he would be early and would have plenty of time to adjust to the sharp voices and clinking glasses at the café, however Geneviève was already there. She was talking with the waitress. He noticed there were at least three tables waiting to be served.

'…and I told him I'd never seen one like it. I said flat out that I wouldn't do it. God knows some people might be curious, but not me,' finished Clotilde.

'You're very wise, Clo,' said Geneviève.

'You wouldn't say that if you knew me better,' laughed the waitress.

'Ah, here you are, Théo.'

'Good evening,' said Théo.

'Another glass,' said Geneviève. She motioned to the waitress who raised her chin a fraction to acknowledge Théo's arrival then disappeared inside.

'Sorry you were waiting.'

'Don't be. Have you eaten?'

'Mama insisted,' he said, raising his eyes slightly.

'Ahh, Théo. Don't you ever get tired of being a gentleman?'

'A what?'

'I have to stop myself cursing in front of the kids. Hugo thinks little enough of me already. I nearly lost it in Petite Marché this afternoon because they had run out of bread – you know how they always run out of bread. Well by then I'd just about had enough of everybody. But you,' she took a gulp of wine, 'you always stay so calm. I wonder though, what are you like underneath?'

The waitress deposited a glass and receipt on the table.

Geneviève fumbled with the screw top of the bottle then poured Théo a generous glass.

'What were you talking about with the waitress?'

'I shouldn't tell you.'

Théo looked across at the tray of drinks being carried between the tables.

'Why not?'

'It was personal.'

'You're in a café.'

'Well, she had a liaison shall we say, with…it doesn't matter who, but he wanted – no, no, I must stop. You don't need to hear this sort of gossip.'

Théo drank his wine and poured another. He wasn't accustomed to such a quick intake of alcohol and it took swift effect.

It still didn't feel quite right being there. He kept thinking about his mother, the cat woman, the girl. He couldn't seem to get his mind off them, like he was reaching some sort of crisis point. He drank and refilled his glass again.

'…I said, "If it's not broken you're going back to school and when you get home you can clean out the pool." He didn't cry the whole time. I felt like such a bitch when I saw the x-ray, but I couldn't stop myself…'

'Geneviève, I have to ask you something.'

'…it was like he had done it on purpose…' she continued.

'You asked what I was like underneath…'

'…like he knew…'

'…truth is, I've never been with a woman, not properly,' said Théo.

'…that his fa– What did you say? Really? Why are you…I can't believe it. So, you've never ha–'

'You have to tell me, Geneviève. Does a woman know?' he said.

'Théo, what are you talking about?'

'Does she know what a man has done? If he's done things?'

'What sort of things?'

'I'm not this man that you see. I'm…you cannot want to know me.'

'Théo, calm down. People are turning around.'

'I don't think I can go on.'

'It doesn't matter, whatever it is,' she said. 'Of course I will want to know you. I can't help you personally in *that* way. And to your question, no, a woman does not know. She has no idea. But not answering your phone when there's an emergency call from your son's school and then denying you were away from work all afternoon tells her a lot.'

'I don't understand.'

'Ignore me. Your difficulty we can work on, mine…I want to forget about. Clotilde, another bottle.'

The waitress nodded from the doorway.

'Clo, do you have time to pull up a chair?' said Geneviève when she returned with the wine.

Théo looked more carefully at Clotilde. It was like he was seeing her for the first tim. He noticed that her brown hands were embellished by a silver ring with a blue oval stone; he noticed her neat wrists, her wrinkled elbows, the darker pigment in the creases by her armpits. He saw her neck and the soft vertical hollow of her clavicle.

Théo forgot the cat woman, his mother and the girl. Geneviéve had told him that his mother was wrong.

He was suddenly moved by the woman in the seat beside him, this waitress whom he'd known for years but never really looked at before. And now Théo didn't want to let her out of his sight.

Irma Lagrasse

Her name was chiseled into the white marble in a formal Roman style, 'IRMA LAGRASSE.' Beneath was the year of her birth and another figure she could not quite read. Lower down in italicized script were three words, *'PRIEZ POUR ELLE.'* There were no offerings, nothing except the simple low stone rectangle separating her designated plot from the dry earth.

She dismissed the vision as unimportant. For one thing it was inaccurate – she would not be buried alone, for another the rectangle seemed insufficient in size. What was the saying? 'A round peg in a square hole.'

The final bars of the recessional hymn stirred her from the reverie.

'Irma. Irma.'

Someone was patting her arm.

'What?' said Irma, opening her eyes. 'What is it now?'

'You looked like you were sleeping.'

Marie gave her a grey-toothed smile. It was less smug than it used to be, less certain.

'Sleeping? Good grief, what did you think I was sleeping for?'

'Your eyes were closed.'

'I was thinking, meditating. Don't fuss about me.'

Marie took the hint, picked up her handbag and began shuffling to the centre aisle.

Irma leaned on the bench crumpling the service sheet in her fist. She pushed downwards and rose to her feet then looked over to where Sandrine was rearranging her music. With perfect pitch Irma hummed the descant to the last hymn that had been unattempted by the congregation. The high notes filled the slow air of the church.

'You were sloppy playing that third phrase,' Irma called over. 'Attention, more attention, Sandrine.'

'I must clear away, Madame.'

'You should sing with more confidence as well,' said Irma.

'I'm concentrating on the music.'

'Pah. You know where the keys are. We've had this hymn a hundred times. It's a wonder I didn't drop-off. Anyway, it's a compliment.'

'Thank you, Madame. Careful. Let me hel–'

'I'm managing perfectly.'

Irma sidestepped along the pew avoiding the wooden feet of the kneeler. She wore cork-soled sandals with a single broad strap. They were unflattering but comfortable. There was a distinct white line around the base of her feet indicating the considerable pressure they were subject to.

She paused when she reached the side aisle, one hand resting on the top of the pew. She looked up at the crucifix and nodded in farewell.

'Suggest something new, Sandrine. Tell him we're all bored.'

'Madame, I couldn't say tha–'

'What a worrier you are. I knew Father Marc when he was putting his shoes on the wrong feet. Poor Father Adibe, what must he think?'

Irma turned away. The trusty pillars beneath her body bent and swung, perambulating her through the double door. She stepped around the bat droppings in the porch into the nook between the church and the street. The door of the presbytery, originally maroon, had faded to the colour of blackcurrant sorbet.

More often than not the Nigerian priest took Sunday mass. He had a voice exactly like marrons glacés it seemed to her, much finer than Father Marc's. In her opinion Father Adibe was too modest in his attempts to sing and preach.

She enjoyed shaking his hand after mass, together their hands were a good fit. His fingers were broad as her own, longer though and black-skinned with a pale palm.

Of course, Sandrine should not be nervous. It was hard to believe that nearing her thirtieth birthday her fingers still trembled as she prepared to play. The first several years of Sandrine's lessons had been directed at correcting her posture and increasing her confidence as much as teaching her piano. There hadn't been any struggle encouraging her musicality once these were addressed.

71

Sandrine had been playing at mass for nearly a year now – hardly a big performance, yet Irma knew it would preoccupy her. From the way she muddled her sheet music afterwards it was still a relief to be finished, yet Sandrine had been the one who approached her.

As Irma walked she remembered how their conversation had run last summer.

'Madame, may I say something?'

'Hello, Sandrine. Of course, what can I do for you? A request?'

'No, Madame. I – I…' Sandrine stopped then began again, 'Well, there aren't too many young people in church.'

'I agree – too many grey heads. Are you disillusioned?'

'No, no. It's nothing like that.'

Irma remembered how Sandrine had looked up sharply at the statue of Saint Paul.

'It is about mass,' she said, when she turned her attention back. 'Perhaps, I might take on some of the burden of playing?'

'Here?'

'It would mean you could sit back, without having to bother about…' Sandrine gestured at the new keyboard, '…all the music.'

'Well dear, you know I don't mind doing it. The instrument doesn't bother me. Better this electric thing than having to climb those damn stairs to the organ.'

Sandrine had glanced up at the apostle again.

'Madame…' she started.

Irma sighed.

'No need to be so subtle. I'll be good about it, of course I will. You may take over as soon as you like.'

'I haven't upset you?'

'No, my dear. Mind to keep the music at home. Everything gets lost in there.'

Irma nodded towards the door of the sacristy.

Yes, admittedly Irma did occasionally close her eyes during the service, but what was there to keep her awake now she was sitting on the bench with old Marie gossiping in her ear.

No, Irma didn't see herself as part of the grey-haired throng, although in truth it wouldn't be many years before her first pupils reached their retirement age – not many years at all.

Irma walked away from the church's pile of stones, keeping to the centre of the narrowing street. She entered the square by the fountain. Today, the circular pond beneath the statue of diving fish was filled with white froth and smelt vaguely of bleach – the overblown response of the municipal authorities to periods of hot weather.

There were plenty of tables available at the café. It had been several weeks since the strange incident with Monsieur Lenoir. The bullet-damaged windowpane had been replaced and Chef Jean was again affably among his customers, yet custom had not fully recovered. Who knew how many guns there were left over from the war still in the town? Certainly her father's gun had been returned to the family after his death during the war, but she had no idea where it was now.

She took her coffee black and without sugar.

Irma thought about the recent death of her grandfather; he had been ninety-six. His decline had been so unwelcome and so gradual that both she and her mother had ignored it almost until the end. Irma hadn't been surprised that her mother, with no one to care for, had died soon afterwards. The three of them had lived together for nearly thirty years. And what had happened in all that time?

Someone passing by brought her back to the present.

'Bonjour, Madame.'

Geneviève was wearing an orange dress. It was pleated over the bust and skimmed over her lean body ending just above her knees; her brown shoulders were bare. Her son Nico was standing at her side. He measured up to Geneviève's elbow and currently had his arm in a sling. At the request of Marie, who was his grandmother, Irma had recently taken him as a pupil. The boy had green eyes with flecks of dark yellow around the iris that gave him a bright amphibian look.

'Bonjour, Madame.'

'Hello, Nico,' she said. 'How's your arm?'

'All right.'

Irma took the small paper parcel from the saucer of her coffee and handed it to him.

'Merci, Madame,' he answered quickly.

Geneviève patted Nico's shoulder and smiled politely. Irma understood that unless eaten quickly and in public the boy might never taste the sugar; Geneviève had been her pupil as a child and Irma knew her well.

Irma recalled her last lesson with Nico just before he had broken his wrist. Nico had asked her a peculiar question. He'd turned sideways, his fingers remaining positioned over the keys.

'Madame Lagrasse, why are you so fat?'

Irma could not remember being asked the question before.

She did remember her mother saying, 'Irma, I don't know why you are so fat. No one else in the family is fat.'

When they were first married she remembered her husband saying, 'I love everything about you. I love every inch of you.'

She remembered her grandfather saying, 'Eat, Irma. For me. Take another spoon.'

They were happy memories.

So, Irma had no ready answer for the inquisitive Nico, nothing pre-prepared. She composed herself and tried to answer honestly.

'It is not because I mind being hungry. On the contrary I quite enjoy that feeling – I doubt you do.'

The boy shook his head.

'It is not because I am greedy. You see,' she gestured at the room around her. 'How would you describe the room?'

'Plain,' replied the boy after a moment's thought.

'I am fat,' said Irma, 'because I am determined to be fat. Does that answer your question?'

'Determined, Madame?'

'Yes. As you must be to learn this instrument.'

The boy nodded then breathed a short sigh.

'With the left hand this time,' she resumed. 'One finger at a time. Tiptoe over the keys.'

The boy had returned to his lesson. His efforts were never likely to produce the medicine to heal the rift between his mother and grandmother, but Nico was not aware that this was the true purpose of his lessons. If he was, Irma thought it unlikely that it would change his application or success.

Back in the square, before Geneviève stepped away from the table Irma spoke to the boy.

'Open the wrapper. I've decided to take one,' she said. 'That's it, you crunch up the other two.'

Nico opened his mouth and poked in the cubes of white crystal revealing the worn down stumps of baby teeth.

Irma contemplated the square as Geneviève and Nico walked away. She saw that the door of the fishing tackle shop was ajar. 'Lugs' was tapping his fingers on the wooden counter, staring blankly out of the doorway.

It wasn't a day to be sitting. The heat, which made most people idle, made Irma restless. She left her drink half finished and dropped a handful of coins on the table.

She moved like a sailor on a pontoon, flat-footed and wary of the sudden stillness of the ground. Onlookers would have described her as something more immense, a whale or an elephant seal. But at this moment, Irma felt more like an ant, seeking here and there on light pin-legs, probing the air with antennae. Yet still she could not clearly determine where she should be going. Everyone seemed to be turning into doorways or somehow going out of sight. It was a trail she was searching for, a trail that sometimes came and went and occasionally went dead.

Today the trail took her though the somnolent centre of town, past the pharmacy, past the immobilier and its window full of houses for sale. She arrived at the foot of Pont Jeune on the heels of a man in sunglasses carrying a red shoulder bag out of which poked the head of a small dog. It was the kind of thing her brother-in-law would sell in his awful pet shop.

Across the road there was another exit at an acute angle to the bridge, almost heading back underneath it. There was a sign for a neighbouring hamlet and two local signs, black writing on mustard yellow background, one for the cemetery, the other for the hydroelectric plant.

Irma stalked across the road, an ant now in pursuit of something definite. She passed the buzzing, sloshing housing of the turbine and reached the blue metal gate of the cemetery. The hinges shrieked, as she knew they would. They never liked being disturbed.

Inside, a pair of tall pine trees gave the place a slightly Mediterranean air. The cemetery was dusty and dry, separated from the river by a high shoulder of limestone. A pair of green watering cans waited by the public tap.

Irma climbed the meandering slope to the upper levels undeterred on her pilgrimage to the Lagrasse family. She could see the foundations of earlier graves bisected by new edifices. The occasional grave had notices from the town mayor stating the plot was a candidate for demolition and reuse – it would eventually happen to the Lagrasse tomb.

The tomb's surface was like an angular marine mammal, eternally beached and pinned with strange colourful brooches, carved with mysterious letters. Her father was pictured in his army uniform on a horse, a proud cavalryman with a career cut short in the Ardennes. Her mother was second cousin to her father and could have been mistaken as a sister to her grandmother their photographs were so similar.

The image of her grandfather, who had delighted in feeding her butter on a spoon, was the most alive. His bright blue eyes stared out of the picture. He was wearing a crisp white shirt, open at the throat, his tanned neck showing and the occasional escaped hair from his chest. The anarchic white hair was like her own, impossible to wear any way except short.

Irma's double-portion sized body would be the last in the tomb.

She would *not* lie side by side with her husband. After all, she'd only been married to Thierry Miteux for five years. He'd been killed in a road accident just outside Carcassone.

In her mind the marriage did not confirm a position of close companionship in death. In fact even before Thierry died her pupils had only ever changed from calling her Mademoiselle Lagrasse to Madame Lagrasse. She'd not corrected them. No, she would not be buried as Irma Miteux; the name did not fit.

Her body was becoming stressed, unable to dissipate the heat, but she stood stolidly looking at the ceramic flowers, reading the familiar names.

Two weeks later her lessons with Nico resumed. Perhaps emboldened by the sugar cubes and their previous private conversation he asked her another question.

'Madame Lagrasse, when are you going to die?'

'To answer your question I will ask another. Do I look old?'

'No, Madame.'

'But I am old, as old as your grandmother – we were in the playground together. The fact is I have not decided when I will die. Now tell me, why are you unhappy?'

He looked at her blankly for a moment.

'I just am.'

'Do these three things and you will be happy: tell your mother you love her, tell your grandmother as little as possible and eat butter whenever you can.'

The boy nodded gravely.

'And in return for this advice, for me, you must smile three times a day.'

'Is that all?'

'That's all,' said Irma.

'Why don't you play in church anymore?' said the boy.

'I kept falling asleep…my heart wasn't in it.'

'I want you to do it. You're better.'

'Sandrine suffers from nerves. She will improve. Didn't she look after you?'

'Yes. When I was little,' said Nico. 'She won't get better.'

'I can see you are a determined little boy. I respect that. Now, tell me why did you break your arm?'

'It was an accident.'

'No, the truth. It wasn't to get you out of piano practice was it?' said Irma.

'No, Madame.'

'And you could have avoided the accident.'

'Yes, Madame.'

'The truth?' said Irma.

'I was feeling angry,' said the boy.

'And are you still angry?'

'Yes.'

'But you feel better.'

'Yes.'

'And your mother,' said Irma.

'She is angry.'

'But not with you.'

'No. Mostly my father, sometimes with Grandma.'

'That is perfectly okay. Do you feel your wrist is recovered? I suppose you have been playing football?'

'I…'

Nico looked sideways over the wooden rail that separated the music room from the lower part of Irma's sitting room.

'Never mind. We'll make this the last run through, okay? Both hands. Light. Soft.'

It seemed that the boy might play well. Of the things that might get in the way the most troublesome would be his grandmother's enthusiasm that he learn. The broken wrist showed the boy's tactical awareness.

When Nico had finished playing she closed the piano lid then lifted down a saucer from beside her.

'What's this? I'd forgotten I had put it in there. You'd better have it. Enjoy them before your mother arrives.'

The boy bit the marzipan fruit in half. He swung his legs, wobbling the piano stool.

Irma looked at the photographs on the piano. In her mind there rose a noisy chatter of ideas and thoughts about the boy. They were an opinionated lot!

Together they waited for his mother to arrive.

'Madame Lagrasse, he will catch up with his playing,' said Geneviève on the doorstep.

'I should hope so,' said Irma.

'Everything is repaired.'

'And you?'

'Me?' said Geneviève. 'Oh, I'm at my mother's address.'

'Back in the old neighbourhood?'

'I suppose you could say that. I hope he is good during his lessons.'

'Very good.'

'I'll stay if you need me to, but I have erran–'

'No need. We are becoming firm friends.'

Irma looked at the boy steadily. He had the sense to keep his gaze lowered to his shoes.

Irma resolved that if she had the chance to sit next to his grandmother on Sunday she would take it. At least then if she fell asleep it would be an irritation to the old gossip. A long time ago the two of them had been friends. Hard to believe that it was forty years since Marie had ordered the gilt-edged mirror from Carcassone, and Thierry had gone to collect it for her.

All this time and Marie didn't think Irma knew, but she did.

The conversations with her pupils had been informative over the years; the doctor's son; the mechanic's daughter; the gendarme's niece. Irma always treated them as equals, which they enjoyed, and they talked to her. Of course she could never *make* them do anything, but they could be influenced one way or another.

Geneviève had been good at listening and it was never hard for her to recognize her mother's faults. As the years passed, the elegant Marie had lost her popularity in the town; she'd become thought of as over-ostentatious.

Teaching Nico was a final creamy morsel, rich and delicate. Life was full of moments to be savoured; perhaps this was the reason Irma had grown so fat.

Journey Back Home

Why is there always such a hurry?

'Time for the toilet,' he says.

'I don't need to.'

I turn my back. I'll be okay in a minute – when my arm feels less sore.

'Come on, Eddie. Now's a good time to go. Don't start the taps. Sit down. We'll wash hands afterwards.'

I manage a trickle. I look behind into the bowl. The water at the bottom is brownish.

'You need a glass of water with breakfast, Eddie.'

'Water?'

'Don't you worry. I'll pull these up. They're still clean.'

He puts in the plug and runs the taps fast. I prefer it when the drops dribble in a slow stream down the plughole.

'Put your hands in. Nice and warm for you.'

The place where he squeezed aches, but I like the water. I float my fingers on the surface. They are surrounded, gripped by the up-swinging lip of the water's skin. I imagine the pink bowls of my fingertips pressing into the wateriness beneath.

He presses the dispenser twice. Phluk-phluk. Peach-coloured goo blobs onto the cracks between my fingers. There is not nearly enough to make a proper amount of bubbles.

'Rub them together.'

He tries to sound encouraging. I deliberately let the soap dribble through. He grips my wrists, dunks my hands under the water. My shirtsleeves get wet.

'All done,' he says.

We go downstairs. I sit at the table and wait for him to come back.

'It's hot. Give it a blow.'

The porridge is steaming; I lift the spoon to my lips. It burns my tongue.

'I told you it was hot. Have a drink of water.'

'I don't want water.'

'I could get you some milk? Warm or cold?'

His hand is resting on the shoulder of the milk bottle with a green lid. His nostrils are flaring slightly.

'Warm,' I say.

'Can I have some honey?' I ask.

'It's in already,' he says without looking around.

It's not raining outside, there's no sunshine either, just trees swinging slowly against the sky. They look giant. How did they get so tall? He turns around muttering something.

Soon he comes back. I drink the lukewarm milk and have a few spoons of porridge.

When I leave the table I go into the next room. Standing still I run my fingers over the surface of a piece of furniture. There are places that are worn – corners, edges – where it is possible to feel the grain beneath the varnish. I rub my finger over the keyhole, feel the chill of the metal surround. I move my hand to the edge of the diagonal slope. I try to lever open the flap.

'It's tight shut,' I say out loud.

Nobody's listening. I look at the thing again. Must have a name. Everything's got a name. I want to ask someone, but there's no one around.

'Won't you come out, Teddy?'

She's holding the back door open, the woman with short grey hair and brown eyes.

'I've got a few minutes today. I'll peel some potatoes, get them ready so you can have a proper meal.'

'Can I go in the garden?'

'It's your garden. Remember you told me, "It's a young man's soil"?'

'What?'

'Clay soil. Oh, never you mind. Watch the lip of the door. That's it, hold me.'

I catch my toe. My face lurches forward. I must look like a hen poking its head out of a coop. She steadies me, pats my hand. It's a reassuring sort of touch she has. I look into her face. She's got a nice wide mouth, some hairs on the top lip, even so I like her smile.

There's a sweet scent outside, high and musty.

'What are those?'

'Oh, I don't know,' she says. 'Smells of honey. See it's brought the bees over.'

They float like dots before my eyes over the low white flowers. They must have a pretty name. A pretty name for a pretty flower. She leads me to a sun-faded green plastic chair. I sit and watch the bees.

'Is it my garden?'

Her face appears at the back door.

'What was that?' she says. 'Everything all right, Teddy?'

I nod. When she's gone I get up and walk over to the trees. The leaves are shaped like tridents. I pull one off, hold it, drag my finger over the shiny side. It makes a small sharp squeak. I feel I'd like to make a collection, but there's no bucket or container to put them in.

'Teddy? What have you got?'

I show her the creased fragment.

'A sycamore leaf,' she tells me.

'It's a nice garden.'

'I think you'd better come in now. Won't you come in now?'

The grass is damp and tufty. I look down and see that I am still in slippers. Where are my wellies? I should be wearing wellies to keep my feet dry.

I catch my toe again on the lip. There is steam rising up from a pan on the stove. It's bubbling and spitting out beneath the lid. Globules hiss as they land on the hot electric ring.

She goes over hurriedly and twists a dial.

'How d'you switch it off?' I ask.

'It's not for you Teddy. I'll do any cooking. It's switched off at the wall.'

'I can do eggs,' I say.

I walk past the spitting pan. It's calmer now, but there's froth and mess all dribbled down one side. I get a cloth from the counter and start to mop it up.

'Not with a tea towel, Teddy. Let me do it. Sit down at the table.'

'I'm helping.'

'No, thank you. Will you give it to me? Go sit down. Have a

drink of water.'

There's a plate on the table, a plastic cup with a handle, a knife, fork, spoon, and a bottle of tomato sauce.

'What are we having?' I call.

'You're having potatoes, sausage roll and beans.'

'Can I have tomato sauce?'

'It's on the table.'

I look back and see it's already there. It doesn't say 'Heinz' it says 'Tesco'. Must be a new brand. What happened to Heinz?

She puts my plate on the table.

'You eat up. I'll have a clean round. He'll have done nothing this morning. I'll check your room for laundry.'

I like the sausage roll – pink, greasy, salty meat. It won't cut up so I eat it with my fingers, dipping it in the beans. Orange sauce drops onto the table. I leave the spuds.

'Are we going out later?' I call.

There's no reply. She's not in the kitchen. I prefer it when she's near. I get up and go away from the table. There's a piece of furniture in the next room. I stand by it and run my fingers over the wood. It's got a keyhole.

'Finished already?'

'Made a bit of a mess, sorry.'

'Don't worry. I'll tidy up. Oh, I see.' She looks at my trousers. 'Let's get you to the toilet. See if you've got anything left. You should have called me.'

'What's your name?'

She looks at me.

'It's Maria. Ma-ria.'

'Do you have a badge?'

She smiles. Her voice softens.

'No, I don't have a badge.'

I go with her. I hold the rail by the toilet so I don't slip.

'What were you fiddling with the bureau for?'

'Nothing. Sorry about the mess.'

She puts fresh clothes on me, helps me upstairs and into bed. She closes the curtains so I can take a nap.

When she's gone I pick up the clock. There's a flat button you press to make the light glow and two smaller buttons; one says, 'HOUR' the other says, 'MINUTE.' I press them and the numbers change.

I feel the flat sheet under my hands, all tucked in. My last thought is that my feet are uncomfortable, curled over by the weight of the cover.

It is very light outside when I wake up. I push away the covers then get to my feet. I keep opening doors until I find the toilet. It's pulling-up that's fiddly, gripping the elastic, pulling without standing on the ends. I notice my arm feels sore.

I stand by a window and look down into the garden. There's a black bird on the washing line. 'Sing a song of sixpence a pocket full of rye, four and twenty blackbirds baked in a pie. When the pie was…'

I hear footsteps, jingling keys. Someone calls from downstairs.

'Hello? Edward?'

A woman comes into the bedroom.

'What have you done with those trousers!' she laughs. 'This isn't your usual room, Edward. Have you just woken up?'

'Clock says it's midnight.'

'It needs resetting again. Why would I be here at midnight? It's teatime.'

Downstairs, in my bowl there is green soup. I dip my bread and suck out the warm salty liquid.

'Here's your cup of tea, Edward.'

She places it on the table then folds her arms over her chest. She's got a big chest, like our neighbour Mrs Johnson when we lived in St George's Road – we could hear her bedsprings creak through the wall when she and Mr Johnson were in bed together.

'I shared a room with my brother, Toby.'

'What was that?'

'We had the best cigarette card collection of anyone.'

'Who did?'

'He knew Stan – he was older and would swap cards for biscuits or bread or half a bottle of lemonade. Stan Longbottom – used to train at the boxing club, had one fight when he was blee– '

'More soup? Or a yoghurt?'

'No. I don't want it.'

I was telling her something.

'I'll move the tea to your chair,' she says.

I leave the table and follow. There are four chairs in the other room; one is yellow with extra cushions. There are flecks of dry skin and white hairs where someone's head has rested on the back. I stand nearby a bit of furniture; it's well put together, good workmanship. I reach out to touch it.

'Do you want that open?'

'Open?'

'You're forever hovering by it. I can open it if you like – have a look at your letters and photos and things. Would you like that?'

I can see she doesn't mean it.

'No. I…'

Her bosoms push up and out as she takes a deep breath.

'Your tea's by your chair,' she says.

'Saved my life,' I say, 'the man on the horse. We were caught in the Ardennes. I was left behind after our movement orders changed. I'd thought to get to higher ground – no idea where I was going, but then I hear hooves. Captain Lagrasse, he…'

She points to the yellow seat.

'You sit here, Edward.'

'…doesn't seem right that he died.'

She presses the remote controllers and a police programme comes on, then she walks out of the room.

The television is still on. It is dark outside. Someone is letting themselves into the house with a key.

'Time to get you upstairs, Eddie. That's the way. Let's get on with it.'

'I can't switch it off.'

'Don't worry I'll do it.'

Upstairs we're in the bathroom for only a short time.

'Not too bad today, Eddie. Teeth now.'

My teeth are out; clothes off. I'm wearing pyjamas with stripes on and sitting on the side of the bed.

'I wanted to do something.'

'Too late now. Do it tomorrow.'

'Is that it?'

'End of another day for you. Lie down.'

He switches off the lamp. In the dark I reach out and press the button on the clock. The light comes on.

'Don't fiddle with your clock,' he calls from by the door. 'Good night, Eddie.'

'Good night.'

It seems polite to say something back. He goes downstairs, locks the front door and leaves.

I twist my feet sideways and turn to the wall. There's flowers on the wallpaper, like when I was a little boy – but they were deeper blue. I used to peel up the edges where they were hidden by the side of the bed. Mum went mad when she found out. But even that night she came in and kissed me goodnight, always a kiss, a wet little mark on my forehead; always called me her 'little man.'

I remember so clearly – those flowers on the wallpaper.

After the Afternoon

The experiment at debauchery left Geneviève calm; a sensation of physical alignment overcame her. Alongside this, and cohabiting quite naturally, was her anger, sharp and red.

She felt in tune with the gush of the river, there was even something pleasant about the droning hum of the hydroelectric station as she drove past. The vibration of the car wheels synchronized with her senses.

The threads of disbelief and wounded pride, which had initially been so prominent when she'd discovered her husband's infidelity, no longer felt so important. They had been a natural reaction. She was still angry, but she declared to herself that she was an adult and she should not have been so naïve.

Geneviève had approached Guillaume earlier in the day. She had seen him coming out of the railway station and hurried to intercept him before he reached his car.

He'd chuckled briefly at her suggestion then said, 'Why not? When?'

'This afternoon.'

'That might be difficult.'

'Why? Another appointment?'

'I work,' he said. 'We could be busy.'

'Selling tickets? I doubt it,' said Geneviève. 'It's ground to a halt at the château since the old man died.'

She'd placed her mouth close to his ear.

'Hugo has been unfaithful,' she'd said. 'There'll be no strings.'

She moved away, slipping her hands into the pockets of her sundress, pressing her palms into the hollows between her hips and the shallow curve of her stomach.

'I stop for lunch at twelve,' he said. 'Bring something to eat.'

She had nodded, moved her sunglasses to the bridge of her nose then walked away.

Guillaume had laughed again when she'd undressed in the

caravan, when he'd seen her body.

'What *was* Hugo thinking?' he'd said.

She'd stepped forward, grabbing his wrists and pushing him backwards against the foldout table. His smile had quickly disappeared and become something quite different.

The moment came back to her now; the stripes of light hitting the upholstery of the seating that doubled as their bed; the wine on his breath that covered up the other scents in the caravan.

In the past Geneviève had scoffed at one of her female friends who'd been intimate with Guillaume.

'He's so respectful, so natural,' Sonja had said. 'You forget where you are, and he lets you talk and talk.'

'But is he listening?' said Geneviève.

'Yes, I think so. Anyway, it's cheaper than a psychiatrist or an osteopath, I'll tell you that much.'

Guillaume had earned a reputation with women.

Geneviève had seen the way he behaved with men, idling by the fountain or having drinks at Café Rose. He was not outspoken or boorish, never at the centre of conversation. Not that he was shy; he held his own. He had no need to show off – he was like a rich man, comfortable in his own wealth.

Driving away Geneviève was struck by the strong urge for a cigarette, her second of the afternoon, but she wasn't confident anymore in her knack of driving and lighting-up. And the boys would notice when she picked them up from school. They were an observant pair, particularly Nico.

She'd underestimated Nico.

Looking back, Geneviève could see that Nico had been showing signs that something was wrong for weeks, long before he had broken his arm. He'd started whinging about playing computer games and refusing to go outside, or on other days he'd stay outside for hours without even pestering his brother Sebastien for company. He'd just fiddle around pushing cars, making endless grooves in the dust. He would only come back in the house when she demanded he do so because it was time to eat or sleep.

One evening Sebastien had come to her.

'Where's Nico?' he'd said.

'In the garden playing.'

'What are you doing?'

'What does it look like? I'm reading the paper.'

'It's dark. I'll go and find him.'

'If you want,' she'd said. 'I'm going to serve dinner.'

She had set four places, her seat facing Hugo, the boys across from each other. During the meal Nico had choked on his food.

Sebastien had raised the alarm.

'Nico! Nico's choking!'

Nico's neck straightened and tightened, his chin pulled down and back as the muscles in his throat contracted and tried to expel the blockage. Hugo had grabbed Nico's arm, pulled him close and delivered a sharp slap between the boy's shoulder blades.

'Spit it out!' said Hugo.

A grey-pink bolus the size of a golf ball tumbled in a sticky macerated mess onto Nico's plate. It was something that hadn't happened since he was a toddler.

'What did you think you were doing putting that much food in your mouth!' said Hugo.

Nico had said nothing. Geneviève tidied the table and replaced Nico's plate.

A bright red flush covered Nico's cheeks. It went all the way up to his ears, showing the brightly sun-bleached strands around his hairline. He'd stared at his plate, his watery eyes seeming to recede more deeply than was natural after having bulged so excessively. For a moment Geneviève had thought he was going to be sick. He wasn't, but neither did he eat anything else during the meal.

Afterwards Nico had gone directly to the bathroom. Geneviève had found him lying on his bed dressed in pyjamas, staring at the ceiling. She had thought nothing of it, nothing at all of the whole incident at the time.

She was certain now he'd already suspected what Hugo was doing.

Geneviève took a detour from the main road, parking near the old factory site on the far side of the bridge. The bridge had a single carriageway, wide enough for the small goods vans that had gone to and fro across the water. Now, it was hardly used.

The broad iron struts reminded her of the town's meagre industrial heritage. The link between work and the land had waned as the factory grew; now the factory was gone. The trees grew thick and unharvested, the people remained, and sometimes she wondered what *was* the point of it all.

Geneviève walked over the sheets of steel bolted to the bridge's frame. In places corroded spyholes looked down on the green river. She imagined blunt-ended trunks stripped to their greenwood, floating downstream as they had in the past.

Over the bridge she stopped in the shade of a browning sycamore. There were a few minutes to spare before school finished. She lit a cigarette and made a leisurely examination of the houses lining the river. They had become more desirable than the properties within the old centre of town although her mother still derided them because they overlooked what had been the neighbourhood sewer.

Geneviève recollected that one belonged to her friend Théo's parents. She owed Théo an apology. In fact she owed several of her friends apologies.

She could see, could judge quite plainly, that her behaviour *had* become erratic. She was drinking more, smoking, spending. Anything she saw and wanted she gave in to, anything at all. A shopping app that Sebastien had installed on her phone made it so easy. This week she had already bought the boys a kayak, amongst other things.

She wondered if she should get Guillaume anything. He had practically nothing, but then he needed nothing; a bed; some smokes; a woman.

She shook her head. He didn't even have a functioning shower.

All she wanted was a proper shower, but she couldn't have one – not since she'd moved back to her mother's house. Not after she'd thrown her house keys at Hugo and kicked in the side-panel of his car (which had very nearly broken her toe).

'I won't come back!' she'd said. 'Not if you beg me. I've had it with you.' She gestured towards the house and cars. 'All this is nothing to me.'

'Be reasonable,' Hugo had said.

'Why should I? You're a pig. A pig! Where were you when

Nico broke his arm and the school called? Not at work!'

She had walked around in tight circles on the driveway, not because she wasn't serious about leaving, but to give Hugo another opportunity to plead.

'Okay, I'm a pig,' he'd said. 'But you're impossible. You are an impossible woman to live with.'

She'd sworn at him, got in her car and driven away. She'd ended up in her mother's narrow street.

There had not been a warm welcome.

'You can't leave it there,' her mother had said.

'What?'

'The car. It's blocking the street.'

'Since when did you care?'

'Put that drink down and go and move the car.'

Geneviève took another gulp of Pastis.

'Go and move the car,' her mother had said, more strictly. 'And look in a mirror. You need to fix your face.'

Geneviève clamped her teeth together like she had as a teenager. She managed to stop herself from telling the old woman to go fix her own face. Being sanctimonious never suited her mother. However worthy she tried to be she hadn't always been so in the past and Geneviève knew it.

That evening the boys had moved into their grandmother's house. They didn't seem to mind that there was no shower or that they saw Hugo less often. They showed no desire to talk about the reason for the move.

Maybe a bath was better, maybe that way she would feel properly clean, more like herself. For her sense of self had started drifting, like some sort of regression was taking place – or was it a movement towards who she really was? Was the woman she'd become just a construct?

Geneviève flicked away her cigarette. With a few taps on her phone she began searching for 'showers' while she walked towards the school. She remembered to watch her step around the empty cat bowls outside Madame Crébor's. Three animals reclined proprietorially on the shaded windowsill. One was a monstrous ginger tom, the colour of a bowl of apricots. The second was blue-grey, longhaired and had an expression of long-suffering that reminded Geneviève of her mother. The third was more feral, ginger in the main but striped and mottled with blotches of white and black. It was long and thin looking, limp as a rag, hardly able to muster the energy to lift its head to watch Geneviève as she walked past.

What did Madame Crébor do all day? Not polishing tables like her mother, or watering geraniums wearing cotton garden gloves; not running a campaign to re-instate the abandoned library or reading the damn newspaper from cover to cover.

Mind you, thought Geneviève, she'd taken to buying a paper after dropping the boys at school.

She'd resigned just over a year ago. Suddenly, it had just seemed like the right thing to do. Hugo had been going to bed when she'd told him.

'Why now?' he'd said. 'Why not before? Surely, when they were babies it would have made more sen–'

'Sebastien already has handball and swimming, he's talking about some sort of computer club. Nico will have the same. Work doesn't fit in.'

'Can't Sandrine take care of all of that?' said Hugo. 'Isn't that what I pay her for?'

'She's not a taxi. I know they love her, but the boys are older now as well.'

'Is it something else?'

'No, it's not something else. I've been working nearly twenty years.'

'Well. I can't stop you,' he'd said.

Hugo had paired his slippers and taken off his dressing gown.

He kept his body covered more than he used to. Patches of skin on his elbows and chest had become mottled, white and pink like the tip of a mouse's nose. A completely harmless condition the doctor had told him, de-pigmenting of the skin caused by a random change in melatonin production, quite common actually. It was not even unsightly really, yet in the dark Geneviève was aware when her fingers touched these bleached areas, some subtle memory related what she had seen to what she touched. She imagined the texture was strange, even though there was in fact no difference at all. Perhaps she over-compensated for how off-putting she found these areas. Perhaps she touched or caressed them too often, too gently, because when her fingers were there, even if by accident, Hugo's body tensed, subtle but definite, like a fly stretching a spider's web.

Perhaps it *was* something else. Perhaps she *had* needed her work; the detail, the certainty of numbers, their neatness, their obedience, the application of rules.

Geneviève's finger hovered above the 'Buy now,' button on her phone.

'Hello, Geneviève,' said a familiar voice.

Geneviève looked up. Sandrine slipped into step at her side.

'Nico all better? What bad luck that was, but children heal so quickly.'

'He received your card,' said Geneviève.

'Good, and I heard that…Oh, is that a new bathroom?'

Sandrine looked at the screen.

'Do you like it?'

'Better than something above the bath. Didn't you stay in a hotel with a wet room?'

'Yes,' said Geneviève, replacing the phone into her bag.

Even in the summer the au pair's skin remained milk-white. A handful of days at the lake and Geneviève bronzed, her hair became sun-streaked. Sandrine's hair was dark and straight, always swept into a ponytail.

They reached the school and stood for a moment in silence.

'Who are you collecting?' said Geneviève.

'Laura Lentier,' said Sandrine. 'Only a few more pickups.'

Geneviève started.

'What did you say?'

'The end of term.'

'Of course,' said Geneviève. 'I hadn't thought,' she added half to herself.

There wouldn't be many opportunities to visit Guillaume in the holidays – if she decided to go again.

Geneviève was taken back to a sharp moment of fulfilment perched on Guillaume's knee, keeping balance with one hand against the flyscreen while the other held tight to the damp curls at the base of his neck.

She smoothed a hand over her sundress then said to Sandrine, 'Are you working for Lentier all summer?'

'Off and on,' said Sandrine. 'They're travelling. On a cruise I think.'

'Would you mind if I gave you a call?'

Sandrine bent her head a little as if she were thinking about the request.

'All right,' she said. 'I couldn't guarantee anything.'

'No, of course not,' said Geneviève. 'Here they come.'

From behind the thick double door came the scuffle and chatter of children.

Geneviève stepped back slightly. There was a clink of metal and the bobbing bustling stream of children flowed out. The smallest children were first. Sandrine soon had mousey Laura Lentier by her side. She was adjusting a backpack more securely onto the girl's narrow shoulders when Geneviève caught sight of Nico's sandy hair.

'Nico! Here, it's Mum.'

'Hey, Mum.'

He held out a sweatshirt then caught sight of Sandrine and Laura.

'Say "Hello", to Sandrine, Nico. Wasn't it nice of her to send you that card? Show her your plaster.'

'I want to go.'

'Don't pull me like that. I said…'

'It's okay, Geneviève,' said Sandrine. 'I expect he wants to go home.'

Geneviève looked from Sandrine back to Nico. He lowered his eyes and dragged the toe of his shoe back and forth over the pavement.

'Stop that!'

'Really, it's okay,' said Sandrine. 'It's not worth any trouble. You're just tired aren't you, Nico?'

Nico didn't reply. He pushed his shoulder against Geneviève's arm, nudging her away.

'I don't know why you're being so rude, Nico!'

He looked up at her.

She'd never seen Nico's eyes so dark, like thunderclouds before a summer storm. His gaze darted to Sandrine.

Now, Geneviève began to understand.

'Come on, Laura,' said Sandrine. 'Goodbye, Geneviève.

Goodbye, Hu–'

She had nearly said it; she had nearly let it slip out.

'Nico.'

Sandrine corrected herself quickly, but if Geneviève had needed any confirmation of what she had only just suspected she had it now. Sandrine hustled Laura away through the crowd.

Geneviève held Nico's hand. They stood together like lampposts, surrounded by the home time rush.

Sebastien came out of the doors, bouncing a basketball at his feet.

'All right you two. I'm starving.'

As the ball hit the ground Geneviève remembered Guillaume; back arched, eyes wide. As soon as the ball was back in Sebastien's hands the image disappeared.

'Come on, boys,' said Geneviève. 'I'll get you something at the café.'

'Really?' said Sebastien.

'I've got piano,' said Nico.

'No, that's tomorrow. Anyway, I heard you tell Grandma that you hated it. Too hard is it? Perhaps some things *are* too hard. I was never a good judge. I would never listen.'

'I don't mind it.'

'Good. Come on,' said Geneviève, drawing breath. 'I need to speak to you about packing.'

'Packing?' said Sebastien.

'Packing-up from Grandma's,' she said, her words rushing on. 'It's been great staying there hasn't it? And well, you know that your father and I, we needed some time apart. Yes, I know what you're thinking, but it *has* done us some good. I think he'll have been missing us all like crazy and he won't want to start any more fights. With the summer holidays coming you should be at home where there's a proper garden.'

Geneviève paused. Yes, she *was* sure, she had never mentioned that particular hotel to Sandrine. Hugo must have told her, perhaps he had even *taken* her there. No wonder she had hesitated about the summer.

'Boys, I've plans for some building work. Do you think you could put up with that? I'm going to have wet rooms put in.'

'Cool,' said Sebastien. 'Even for us?'

'Yes.'

'What's a wet room?' said Nico.

'You have a big shower and a drain, but it's all open. There's no curtains or anything. I'll show you some pictures.'

'What about Grandma?' said Nico.

'You can go whenever you like, spend the whole day while I sort out the builders. But we'll all move back home. Surely you've been missing your rooms, your toys and things. I mean, Grandma hasn't even got a shower.

'Here we are,' she said. 'That bouncing is driving me mad, Sebastien. Put the ball away. Take a seat.

'Nico, look at me. Hey, try and smile. Dad'll see how he's missed us. He *must* have been lonely. It will be a great big surprise for him. We'll be there all the time.' Geneviève pushed the menu over to the boys then reached into her bag. 'Go on, order whatever you like. I need a cigarette. I know you don't like it boys, but I've hardly sat down all afternoon.'

Dead End Pet Shop

Jonah tapped on the glass and watched the lizard flinch. A small handwritten sign saying 'Mervyn,' had been stuck on the tank lid. There were printed facts telling him that the lizard came from southeast Australia and was twenty years old, and might live twenty more. In large letters were the words, *'Blue-Tongued Lizard. DO NOT TAP ON THE GLASS.'*

Jonah couldn't see a price sticker.

Since there was no one at the counter he knocked again on the glass, harder this time, with his knuckles. Twenty shitty years staring at dog chews might even be worse than his life.

Mervyn's head jerked towards him. His black bubble eyes had a mean look.

'C'mon stick your tongue out.'

The folds of skin under the lizard's chin were crinkled like an old woman's. A drab grey and green pattern spread from its forehead along its back and down to a whip-slim tail. The eyes blinked with bored insolence.

Jonah lifted his hand again to knock on the glass to try and get a performance. One of the lizard's eyes trained on the movement of Jonah's fingers the other stared into the mid-distance of the shop.

The stocky woman with grey hair who'd spoken to him earlier, plodded past and stood behind the counter. She pushed a receipt onto a spike by the till and then glanced in his direction. Jonah put his hand back in his pocket.

'They're getting the puppies out in the yard. You might as well go and have a look while you're waiting for Monsieur Miteux.'

Jonah left the unblinking lizard behind the glass and headed for the double doors at the back of the shop. The sharp smell of fish food caught in his throat as he passed the aquatic section. He held the back of his sleeve against his nose to protect himself from the smell then pushed the door open and stepped outside.

The triangular concrete yard was half the size of the shop. Green netting had been stapled to the fence along one side to provide some shade. The narrower section by the main road had been fenced off into three small compartments. These contained identical knee-high kennels that housed the young dogs. On the right an eager golden Labrador stumbled as it was released from the enclosure into the wider space while two terriers yelped in the centre as they waited for their turn to be let out.

A girl in an oversized 'Petland' T-shirt unhooked the gates. Her arms were white and looked like they would bruise easily. She had bluish make-up smudged over her eyes. She closed the doors behind the terriers then began talking to a man and a woman standing with their back to him.

'They're very friendly. I'll pick one up so you can stroke it if you like.'

The woman in front of him sidestepped carefully to let one of the dogs get past her feet and watched to make sure it moved safely away. She had round shoulders like his French grandma. The bloke turned his head and smiled. It was a broad unrestrained smile, like you'd watched something funny on TV or seen someone walk into a lamp post and you just couldn't help how good it made you feel.

The man stayed staring and smiling at the same spot until the Petland girl held up one of the terriers and started showing him how to stroke it. The old woman reached out and guided the man's hand onto the dog's head.

Jonah found it easy to watch them. It irritated him when a shrill scream distracted him from the scene. It was from a small girl dressed completely in pink. She drew breath to scream again.

She was laying it on thick, stamping her feet up and down and squirming away from her mother.

'Bad doggy!' she cried.

'He's just a puppy,' said her mum. 'I don't think he liked the way you stroked him.'

'Doggy did it!'

'Shh. Come and have a cuddle.'

The mother was saying all the right things, but Jonah could

see she didn't mean it. He could see she hated being in the pet shop, and that she wasn't too fond of the little girl either.

Probably poked it in the ear, he thought. It was always tempting, and dogs really hated it, or maybe she got a handful of fur and gave a good jerk.

The golden Lab had run as far from the noise as it could and was sniffing around by the doors. It stopped and turned, then lowered its haunches and squeezed a round wet turd onto the concrete.

The toddler looked calmly over her mother's shoulder and kept screaming. Her little grey eyes scanned his face, monitoring the effect.

If it had been his sister he would have pinched her. It made her shut up. No one noticed an extra bruise on her scrawny little arms, it just added to the collection of bigger bruises from their dad.

The disabled bloke fumbled with the wriggling animal he'd been given. It yowled in pain as its back hit the floor.

'Careful where you step,' said the old woman, reaching for her companion's arm. 'It's still by your feet. You don't want to hurt the little fella.'

Jonah guessed it was the Petland girl's job to scoop up the shit and keep the kennels clean. She stood watching the puppies scratching around the floor, her arms folded around her skinny waist. She caught his eye.

'Do you wanna' look at one?'

'Nah.'

'They're pretty cute.'

'I guess.'

He felt one of the terriers tugging at the frayed bottom of his jeans. He could see the soft pink skin under the white hairs on its belly as it gnawed at the cotton threads. The toe of his shoe lifted from the floor. Without thinking he almost gave in to the urge to cause an easy injury.

'Thinking of getting one?' asked the girl.

'My dad wouldn't have it.' Jonah answered, shifting his feet. His dad kept lizards, boxes full of them stacked all around the place. He lifted his gaze from the terrier. 'We've got no garden anyway.'

'Flat?'

'Yeah.'

She smiled sort of sympathetically then bent down by his feet. 'I'd better put them back.'

She had a skinny back too, nothing inside her shirt but bones.

She cradled the dog in her arms. The puppy looked at him; bright brown eyes straight into his. It wanted a home. It would trust him forever, whatever he did. Jonah didn't know if he could be trusted like that.

'I gotta go,' he said.

'See ya then,' replied the girl.

She rubbed the dog's neck and held it against her flat chest.

The golden Lab was still hanging around by the swing doors, sniffing and circling around it's little pile of shit.

The cockatoos shrieked as he walked through the shop. It felt stuffy, thick with the warm smell of boiled bones and sawdust. There was so much crap for sale in the place: dog coats, dog shampoo, dog hairbrushes, every bloody thing a dog could want and could bloody well do without.

Old Monsieur Miteux was behind the counter now. He looked up as Jonah approached.

'Are you the lad waiting to see me?'

'What?'

'About the Saturday job.'

'Me? Nah, just havin' a look around.'

The blue-tongued lizard blinked slowly at Jonah.

'Amazing isn't he?' said the old guy.

'Wouldn't know.'

Twenty more years in the tank thought Jonah, twenty more shitty years. He started to walk away, but at the last moment he reached his hand out and flicked the glass hard, making a sharp clink with his nail. Out shot the blue-coloured tongue. It was extraordinary. For a second, Jonah stopped and stared.

Afterwards, he couldn't think why anyone would want to buy the creature once they'd seen it open its mouth.

Outside, his sister Leyla was sitting by the bike racks fiddling with someone's pedals and spinning the chain.

'Dad's been lookin' for you,' she said.

'I'm going to Jacque's,' he replied.

'He won't let you. He said you'd been a little shit and he'd never let you go to Jacque's again.'

'Yeah? He will later, after they've started-up drinking again.'

Leyla stood up and wiped the grease from her fingers onto her shorts.

'What about me?'

Her face was serious, like he knew it would be when she was grown-up.

'I'll take you with me if I can,' he said.

She nodded. They waited together, leaning on the pet shop window, waiting until they were found.

Tiptoes

- 1 -

Vérité had chosen the Jack Russell terrier. He had brown ears, a mostly white body with black splotches on his belly and rump and an inch of ginger at the end of his tail. Of all the puppies in the yard of the pet shop at the end of the deserted Rue Bousculade he was the brightest.

One morning almost a year ago, Eugène had said, 'Vérité, I think Philippe needs a change.'

'A change?'

'Well? Why not? He must be bored.'

Vérité had tousled the dog's ears.

'Philippe, are you bored?'

She had smiled a small sad smile and the decision was made.

The new route tracked past the cemetery and along a quiet tributary of the river into the unpopulated countryside. Their matching white shirts were laid out in the same manner; their departure was still just after breakfast time.

It was cooler beneath the beach trees, their shoes were dirtier. There was a bird whose call sounded like an electric machine malfunctioning that they remarked upon on the first day. Philippe was as bright and content as he always was.

That evening they had sat together in the quiet cave-like sitting room. Eugène adjusted his glasses then said, 'I enjoyed our walk.'

'Yes, yes,' Vérité replied. 'I think Philippe was quite tired out.'

She had looked across to the recliner. The dog's snout rested on the inside of the arm, his tail curled up beneath his back legs. She could see tiny white rounds of teeth between his lips; fine black whiskers grew from his white muzzle.

'We could alternate?' she said.

'No, I don't think there's any need.'

Their old routine had been so established that some of the people who lived along it continued looking up expecting to see them pass at the accustomed time. The lane was quiet and pedestrians were noticeable – once it had been the link between the town and its neighbouring village, but since the construction of the road in the gorge it was effectively a dead end leading to the forest.

Some dog-walkers parked by the auberge de jeunesse then crossed the footbridge over the river directly to the forest rather than walking past the old factory site. However, Eugène and Vérité had always walked from town.

They had got to know the houses on the lane. There was a bed and breakfast run by an English couple with two Alsatians, a summer villa with a small inflatable swimming pool and three badly behaved Yorkshire Terriers, and a house where soup was often cooked at breakfast time.

There was another house, which stuck in both Eugène and Vérité's memory, although neither ever said anything to the other.

Like many properties this particular one had its back to the river and bordered the road directly. At the base of its facade the plasterwork was grey, in some areas flaking away altogether, but higher up it was possible to see the walls had once been painted yellow.

It was a simple dwelling with what looked like a small mezzanine room in the orange-tiled roof. The downstairs windows, of which three faced onto the road, were tallish, with bright-green metal shutters either side. There was no door to the road, but a double gate on one side a little taller than head height. It had been very rare for any of the shutters to be open at the time Eugène, Vérité and Philippe had passed by; although they saw little, sounds could easily be heard: cutlery scraping, clumping feet, banging doors, voices.

'Nothing travels more than the human voice,' Eugène had remarked one day shortly before their change in routine. 'Music, engines, dog-barking gets complained about and so on. But whisper at the back of church or curse by the cash machine, you'll be heard whether you realize it or not.'

He had been reading the newspaper. Amongst other things they had been discussing the amount of money that had been spent on the Bastille Day firework display.

'What a mess it leaves,' Vérité had said. She looked over to the recliner. 'Now, now Philippe, don't you go listening to us. Nothing for you to worry about for a long time.'

The animal had lowered his eyebrows and returned his gaze to the red light on the television.

- 2 -

Bastille Day arrived. The fireworks sounded like a war; first the explosive crack of rockets, then the whoosh, roar, pop of glittering rings and catapulted light.

'He seems fine,' said Eugène, returning from checking on Philippe. 'Half asleep I think.'

'He was awake when I went down,' said Vérité. 'I could feel his heart pounding in his chest.'

'But he wasn't afraid.'

'No. He was being very brave. I told him not to worry.'

They watched the finalé craning at the back window, a tricolour of flowering circles in the smoky black sky preceeded by a cascade of sparks from the walls of the castle. The empty stone keep perched on the low hill rising behind their house and the clank-slosh of buckets soon replaced the fierce noise of the fireworks as their neighbours dampened down embers on the dry grass.

'It's only once a year,' said Eugène.

'I suppose,' said Vérité.

'I think there will have been plenty of people on the bridge,' he said.

She nodded, then went one last time to check on Philippe, as Eugène knew she would.

In the morning everything was bright and clear again. There was mess outside: beer bottles, firework wrappers, take-away containers; it would wait until the municipal clean-up wagon arrived, even then it would take several days for everything to be set straight.

Eugène paused as he was tying his shoelaces. He looked up to where Vérité was tidying her hair in the mirror. She was humming something.

'Perhaps,' he said, '…perhaps it would be a good day to use the old route.'

'The old route?'

'Yes. Avoid the worst of the clear up.'

'As you like,' she said, catching his eye in her reflection. 'Philippe doesn't mind, as long as he gets his walk.'

Together they stepped into the old narrow street, zigzagging down the slope. Along with the rubbish from the Bastille celebrations the gutters were clogged with lime tree flowers dropped by a specimen growing at the base of the castle wall. Many of the old houses had their shutters and windows open to refresh the air inside before being shut again for the rest of what promised to be a hot day.

Eugène and Vérité had always thought they would move, but there had never been need. Philippe was chosen because he would stay small; they managed without a garden.

The dog's relaxed Mortadella-pink tongue trembled as he trotted along by their side, his claws scratching the rounded cobbles as they descended to the broad shoulder of the river. On the opposite bank lay the majority of the town, the old narrow streets and sprawling newer housing.

'Careful, broken glass,' said Eugène, stepping aside.

Vérité picked Philippe up and carried him in her arms until they were well clear.

'Thank you,' she said. 'People can be so thoughtless.'

When they reached the old factory site silence lapsed between them, broken only by the occasional jangle of the medal on Philippe's collar. A pair of red and brown butterflies opened briefly on some buddleia growing through the leaning temporary wire fencing.

The waft of cooking vegetables carried on the air. Eugène and Vérité exchanged a glance and smiled – cauliflower soup, at this time of year!

They passed a red Peugeot; minus a wing-mirror since the last time they had seen it. The wheels had already been visited by several passing dogs. Philippe sniffed, squatted and tensed his white flanks.

Eugène and Vérité passed on ahead.

They paused outside the low house with three windows. Unusually, in the centre the green shutters and window were open. Inside, on the wall directly opposite the window a tie-dyed piece of cloth had been pinned-up. They could see a white cot with its base lowered. There were plastic tubs filled with toys and a half-toppled pile of clean laundry on the floor.

They heard the sound of cutlery from behind the last pair of shutters.

'Why's he taking all day?' said Eugène. 'Philippe?'

'Look, here he is now,' said Vérité.

The dog scampered to heel. As they resumed walking they heard the scrape of a heavy wooden chair on a tiled floor. It was followed by the unmistakable sound of a slap. There was a high-pitched yelp then a woman's voice.

'I told you to put it down! You knew that was going to happen! What a mess. Who's going to clear this up? Eh?'

The shouting ceased, replaced by the low wail of a young child.

As Eugène and Vérité passed the shuttered window the rhythmic crying synchronised with their strides.

'Hungh–hungh–hungh–hungh…'

They could still hear the woman.

'Get down! No more! Your shirt…everything!…it was all clean and now…'

There was another slap.

Eugène and Vérité passed the closed garden gates. Eugène held his breath for a few moments; he kept his eyes fixed ahead seeking the car park sign that he knew would soon appear. Philippe jogged ahead, glancing to check they were advancing behind him.

They reached the car park and headed up the path into the hills. After a while their pace slowed. When his breathing returned to normal Eugène broke the silence, 'Perhaps we could take Philippe to the château tomorrow?'

'A day out?' said Vérité.

'Why not?'

'I was to see Jean, collect his documents.'

'He won't mind the delay. The accounts can wait,' said Eugène.

'You're right. What's that, Philippe? What have you found?' The dog circled the dry body of a snake in the dust. 'Tsk, tsk, come away. You'd think after being bitten he'd leave the things alone.'

'He was only a puppy,' remarked Eugène.

Ten minutes later Eugène looked at his watch. He called Philippe to heel and they began their return. In the dry grass at the edge of the path a cricket began to chirp, the short vibrating call interspersed with the quiet rustle of leaves.

The track widened and they emerged from the trees. They saw a dog and its owner heading towards them. The greyhound loped along, its grey coat shimmering as it moved.

The man stooped and patted Philippe on the back, issuing a simple 'Good day,' to Vérité and Eugène. The dogs inspected each other, but resisted the temptation to play.

Excited by the greyhound's fresh markings Philippe sniffed and pawed the ground. He stopped briefly then trotted ahead and began the process again, this time at the base of a high double gate.

- 3 -

Vérité and Eugène hear the sound of crying. They hear the desperate wet breaths sucked in between the long drawn-out defeated sobs.

Eugène and Vérité walk past Philippe nosying at the bottom of the gate, they walk past the first set of closed shutters, they reach the next pair – still wide open despite the full risen sun. The centre of the room is caught in a bright rectangle of light. They see the cot and the mess on the floor. They see the child, reaching up with its fingers for the door handle, pushing up against the door frame, balancing on tiptoe. One foot hovers above the floor as the fingertips strain to touch the dark metal handle. They see the child tip the handle downwards, sliding her fingers forwards for grip. Then her hand slides off. The handle springs back to horizontal and the child emits a high, wild scream.

'Mama! Outside! Outside! Outside!'

Eugène and Vérité pass on to the next shuttered window. The shouting turns to a pleading lament.

'Mama…mama…'

It is only when they are half a dozen steps past the house that they realize that Philippe is not with them and that he is also no longer visible on the road.

'Where is he?' says Eugène

'Philippe!' calls Vérité. 'Here, boy.'

There is a jangle of metal. Philippe is behind the double gate belonging to the yellow house; they see his whiskers. After an acknowledging bark he runs away.

Eugène and Vérité retrace their steps. Neither looks into the room with the open window. Each hears the sound of the metal handle springing upwards again.

'Philippe, come here!' calls Vérité.

This time there is no bark, no snout peeking under the gate. Eugène steps forward and knocks briskly. He doesn't wait long before reaching over the top and unhooking the latch.

The garden is strewn with faded plastic toys.

'Hello. Anybody here?' he calls. 'Philippe, what are you doing over there?'

Eugène crouches down. The dog runs out from underneath a crooked mini-trampoline and leaps up into his arms.

The wooden door in the side of the building flings open.

'What th–'

'Madame, I'm sorry to intrude. Philippe squeezed under your gate. He's so curious. He got away from us.'

Philippe barks and wags his tail. He squirms in Eugène's arms and is passed to Vérité. The dog strains upwards to nuzzle and lick her chin.

'Yes, yes,' says Vérité, 'telling us all your adventures, aren't you? Goodness me. You should be apologizing. Come on, less of all that nonsense.'

The woman from the house folds her arms over her chest. Her blue cardigan is stained and the grey shirt beneath is wrinkled; both are of good cloth, but hang limply on her body.

'Well, you found him,' she says.

'We'll leave you in pea—'

'Doggy-doggy!'

The little girl stumbles out over the doorstep.

'What? How did you get out?' says the woman.

'Doggy,' squeaks the girl.

'Would you like a stroke?' says Vérité.

She kneels down so the child can reach more easily.

'Watch your fingers,' says the mother.

The woman speaks with a fine accent, not southern, not local.

'You're very friendly aren't you, Philippe?' says Vérité. 'He won't mind if you stroke him. He's six years old, not a puppy anymore.'

The little girl reaches out, she strokes the dog with her palm rather than her fingers, pressing firmly on each stroke. Philippe pants. He turns his head to the girl.

Eugène watches the woman in the doorway. He sees she has freckles, but it doesn't look like she has spent much time outside. She is picking at her lips with one hand.

'Doggy-doggy. Mama, doggy-doggy.'

The girl looks up at her mother then back to the animal. There are still streaks of tears on her cheeks. She licks at the lines of mucus between her nose and top lip.

'Say, "Hello," Philippe,' says Vérité.

Philippe gives a short bark.

'No, doggy! No, doggy!' scolds the girl.

The girl stiffens her fingers, tilts her hand ninety-degrees and draws it back.

'Bad, doggy!'

Eugène reacts more quickly than Vérité. He bends over and catches the girl's wrist, bringing it to a stop before her open hand makes contact with the dog's muzzle.

'He's not being naughty. He's telling you he wants to play,' Eugène says quickly. 'You have a good heart, haven't you, Philippe?'

The woman pulls her daughter away.

'More than can be said for her,' she says. ' "My Little Bitch," I call her. "Bitch. Bitch. Bitch." She doesn't understand. I'm

109

sorry, Monsieur. She's not used to animals.'

Vérité stands up, holding Philippe in her arms.

'Yes, he has a good heart,' she says.

She strokes him on the chest so he sits calmly then kisses him tenderly on the top of the head like a baby.

'He is just a dog,' says the woman.

'Pardon?' says Vérité.

The woman stays quiet, keeping her fingers tight around the upper arm of the girl. Vérité takes Philippe's paw and waves it from the gate. The little girl looks sideways at her mother before risking a grin.

Before Vérité is fully out of earshot the woman says to Eugène, 'She's a bit soft, eh? Your wife.'

Eugène thinks of saying, *'Do you realize that anyone who walks past knows you leave your daughter shut in that room, and have done since she was a baby? You should be ashamed.'* But he does not.

Instead he says, 'No, Madame,' and walks away.

Vérité does not put Philippe down until they reach the purple spikes of buddleia. Crickets are now singing every few yards in the urgent colonizing vegetation. The sun hits a spreading circle of crushed glass on the surface of the road.

Eugène thinks of saying, *'Perhaps we were wrong to give up trying. Perhaps there was still hope.'* But he does not.

Instead he says, 'Yes, I think we definitely deserve an outing – the three of us.'

'He's such a good boy,' says Vérité, '…but, I think coming this way…I think going back to this way…might be too much for him.'

She looks at her husband. Her eyes are wet. He takes her hand and squeezes it gently as they walk side by side.

Inside, Outside

'What's that?'

Laura pointed through the glass. She'd never seen anything like it back in France. Hurriedly, she squirreled around in her seat trying to get a better look before the traffic cleared and their bus moved on.

There was no reply from the older boy sitting next to her. She repeated her question. This time, against her expectation Pierre replied.

'A steam engine,' he said.

'To pull a train?'

'No,' said Pierre. 'Just an engine. Doesn't go on a track, doesn't even move really.'

'But it wants to,' said Laura. 'It's trying to get away, look at it jigging forward all the time.'

Two men with wrinkled faces, one with a flat cap, the other in blue overalls, looked contentedly at the machine. A line of metal stakes supported a line of bright orange plastic netting to keep onlookers at a safe distance. She knelt up to peer out of the window at the contraption.

'For heavens sake, Laura. Sit down!' came a voice from the row behind. 'Turn around properly and get your feet off, or you'll have to swap with Céline and sit next to me.'

Laura sank back onto her haunches so her father could no longer see her. She didn't want to move. She certainly didn't want to sit in a space vacated by Céline, her father's girlfriend.

Laura edged forward and pressed her nose flat on the glass. The window felt like a cold coin on her nose as she scanned the line of engines in the field by the side of the road. In the background, where the two blues of sea and sky met, the horizon was interrupted by the glowing angular mass of the cruise ship to which they were returning.

'What are they for?' she asked over her shoulder to Pierre. 'They must've been for something.'

She could hear him tapping out some sort of drumbeat on his knee. Again in truth, she didn't expect him to answer, but she sensed him lean forward behind her to see.

'Farm jobs,' he replied, 'before tractors and combines…with steam…that's why they've a funnel.'

The bus vibrated deeply and edged forward. Laura heard her father speaking behind her.

'It's a van,' he said. 'It's towing a caravan, trying to turn around. Keeping us all waiting.'

Céline said nothing. Céline often said nothing in reply to her father's conversation.

If they weren't on the bus Céline would be smoking. Céline smoked and nodded, and leaned backwards in her chair in response to almost everything. Laura supposed that since smoking was not allowed on the bus, and it was impossible to lean back in the moulded seats that Céline was reduced to simply nodding.

'What about the tiny one?' said Laura.

'Must have powered something,' said Pierre.

'No, not that one, not the little green one. The *tiny* one on the table. Look he's feeding it with a plastic dropper, like you get with eye-drops. See how mini it is.'

'It must be a model…a train engine. Probably it's paraffin.'

The man feeding the engine flinched and pulled back suddenly. He grinned at a pair of small boys holding dribbling ice creams and shook his hand.

'Must've been hot,' said Pierre.

Laura nodded.

Even from inside the bus she could see that the smaller boy's cone was badly flooded. It only needed a few licks to tidy it up nicely, but the boy was too busy sucking the soft white dome to bother about the rest. She pushed her hand up against the glass.

'Look, a monster,' said Pierre.

'Where?'

'Past where they're selling chips.'

A man was standing on top of what looked like a red wooden fire-engine. He untied a sheaf of wheat then tossed it into a square black mouth like he was trying to pacify a large gyrating animal. A neat stout bale tumbled out of a hatch on one side like a waste deposit.

She turned and grinned at Pierre.

'It would have been good to go in,' she said. 'See everything close up,'

But then she wouldn't have gone into town.

Pierre picked up a grey earphone from where it rested on his knee. He considered her for a moment, then he said, 'I missed you.'

Laura had hoped that her au pair Sandrine would accompany them on the cruise. When her father had told her it was Céline's younger brother coming with them, she had resolved that whatever Pierre was like it would be better than just the three of them.

So far, Pierre had not spoken more than a few words to anyone. Mostly he listened to headphones. He was a teenage; he could do things on his own whereas she was always accompanied or monitored.

Laura occasionally overheard adults saying she was too solitary, but she was actually rarely alone. Not *proper* aloneness, with no one listening or watching for her.

If she were upstairs in the attic bedroom her father would call her.

'Laura, what are you doing? Why don't you come and play downstairs?'

Of course, he didn't really want her downstairs, especially if Céline was there.

If her father thought Céline might find an activity annoying or boring it would not even be suggested.

Céline liked sun bathing, so at home in France they went to the lake.

There were only the smallest triangles of Céline's body that were not the colour of strong English tea. One night when Laura had been about to climb down the attic ladder to go to the toilet she'd seen a small pale triangle floating in the dark below and realized it was Céline's bottom.

Although she'd never told anyone what she'd seen, Laura imagined her mother perched on a stool in her kitchen and speaking into her mobile saying, 'What kind of woman walks about the house naked?'

She'd never seen her mother naked. She couldn't remember her mother removing her bikini top like Céline did, or leaning on her father's chest like Céline did.

Her mother's house was modern and white on the inside, crumbling and ancient on the outside. When Laura stayed there she would play a game called, 'Inside-outside,' by the back door.

She would hop or jump either side of the threshold, chanting, 'Inside, outside, inside, outside, in!' then land as far as she could inside the kitchen. Then she'd reverse the rhyme then leap outside onto the path.

Today, her mother's house seemed a long way away; a long time ago.

Earlier that day, when they'd got off the bus that took them from the cruise ship into town her father had agreed to go to the shops. Laura was certain it was because Céline liked choosing clothes, not because she, Laura, had complained of feeling cold on the ship.

'It's twelve to thirteen years,' her father had said, shaking his head.

Laura shot out an arm and pulled the garment into the cubicle. 'I'll try it.'

'It's too big,' said Céline, motioning for him to try again.

Her father was agitated when he returned.

'Shit,' he'd said. 'There's none left. Just this…what on earth is it? That yellow cartoon thing?'

'Oh, I love it!' said Laura.

'God's sake I'm not paying for that,' he'd said.

'She can try it,' said Céline.

Céline looked past them both, examining her skinny reflection in the wall mirror. She tipped away a stray blond corkscrew.

The feeling of fleece against Laura's arms and legs had been like rolling on soft carpet.

'Wowee! It's so cosy!'

'Okay, you can have it. No more fussing. Unzip it properly. I don't want it wrecked in the damn shop. Get dressed.'

Laura could see the heels of Pierre's neat white trainers

under the bottom of her door when she bent down to pull up her trousers.

Céline and her father had been out of sight when she came out.

For a while Laura wandered around the rails then she'd started playing in the shop doorway. The automatic doors stayed open as long as she kept moving.

'Outside, inside, outside, in!'

The shop girl rearranging clothes didn't notice her. She looked tired anyway, kind of grey and green around the neck and chin. Her eye make up looked like the ground in dirt that Laura's father complained about if he took notice of her washing routine in the bath.

'You can't have washed properly for weeks!' he would say. 'How can you get so dirty? Lather, now scrub.'

'Yes, Papa,' she would say.

There would be no reason to lie about dirt behind the ears she reasoned. What did it matter though? If Céline noticed, she never said anything. Laura thought, perhaps the shop girl does not have a good washing routine.

Further inside the shop, by the rows of men's T-shirts and sweaters Laura could see her father and Céline. She was holding up a shirt with one hand while Laura's father flattened the fabric against his chest.

Laura had squinted to see further back. Pierre was leaning next to a half-dressed mannequin, one foot up on the wall behind him, his hands and eyes engaged with his mobile phone.

'Inside, outside, inside, out!'

Laura collided with the burly frame of a woman wearing a bright orange shirt and sturdy Velcro sandals. The woman's skin was velvet brown, rosy around the cheeks.

'Watch out, girl,' said the woman, smiling. 'I'm goin' to do more harm than good if I step on you.'

Laura hadn't understood what she meant.

She'd mumbled, 'Pardon,' and sidestepped around the grey security bollard.

She liked the woman's crooked teeth, her soft belly and bright eyes. Most of all she liked her bright pink toenail polish. Then to Laura's surprise the woman spoke to her in French with a rich north African accent.

'Cruise ship passenger?'

'Oui, Madame,' Laura answered.

'Tried the ice cream yet?'

'Non, Madame.'

'Well, don't go wasting too much time before you do.'

The woman had smiled and clicked her tongue. She reached out and made contact with Laura's cheek with the pillow of muscle beneath her thumb then turned sideways and ambled out of the shop.

Laura began again.

'Outside, inside…'

But the game was beginning to get boring. Too many people were walking in and out of the shop and they weren't all as friendly as the fat woman in orange.

'…outside, inside, out!'

Laura jumped away from the sliding door, clearing the dimpled tiles that sloped up from the slabs that served as both pavement and road.

The sun fell on her face, cutting sharply across the line of shops that leaned over the road like trees along the river back home. She took a few paces into the triangle of light. The sun pressed warmly on her clothes. She hadn't been able to feel its warmth when they disembarked, hadn't dreamt that it could possibly be the kind of day when she would want ice cream.

Through the vertical bars of some scaffolding Laura caught sight of a flash of an orange shirt. A pushchair moved aside then she saw an advertising board and just behind it a giant plastic model of an ice cream cone. It was as tall as she was and shone like a beacon, reflecting the blue and white sky above.

Laura's hand had bobbed over the metal poles. She hummed the tune of her jumping rhyme as she walked, remembering the special stones that glittered on her mother's path. She wondered if the same stones existed here. The grey slabs seemed so drab and heavy, like dominos laid end to end by a race of giants.

Perhaps, she had thought to herself, there really *were* giants on the island and this was their giant ice cream, stolen and frozen. Laura touched the perfect white turban. The plastic was dry, smooth and warm.

From inside the shop came a fizzing sweet smell and the atmosphere of close-bodied excitement from people crammed into a special museum exhibition.

Laura felt in her pocket and stepped inside.

She had inhaled deeply. A sharp citrus note was followed by a velvety pink sugary scent. On the left there was an ice cream cabinet with a glass front. It was the same design as in Café Rose back home, except there were bright blue plaques and the yellow lettering described the flavours in English. What really interested Laura though was the stout metal box whirring gently above her head. On the side of the machine was a sticker of a smiling ice cream cone and writing saying, 'Mr Whippy.'

She hadn't been sure how to pronounce 'Whippy.' When her turn came in the queue she'd said, 'One ice cream, please.'

'Flake?' said the shopkeeper.

She was confused for a moment then saw the tray of stout lengths of crumbling chocolate.

'Oui. Yes, please.'

The metal box burred more deeply for a few seconds. The shopkeeper held out the cone and Laura held up her coin.

'Euros? No, I can't take them. You need to pay in pounds,' he said.

'Je n'ai pas…' she began, shaking her head. 'Je n'ai pa–'

'Don't worry yourself,' interrupted a voice speaking in French. The woman in the orange shirt smiled down at her then said in English, 'I'll pay for her.'

She passed the cone down to Laura then gave over some silver coins to the shopkeeper. Laura noticed that each of the woman's fingernails were painted a different shade, like they'd been dipped in a box of jellybeans.

'Go on, take a lick before it melts,' said the woman.

'Merci, Madame,' said Laura.

Laura had performed a sort of bow, her hot cheeks coming close to the shiny, drippy, ice cream. She walked out gripping her two-euro coin in one hand and the ice cream in the other.

Laura licked carefully all the way around the cone then up to the chocolate flake. She kept her eyes down, following the flow of the stone slabs. She started to appreciate that each one *was* different; some glinted; some had delicate impressions like bird tracks; others were smooth as pebbles.

Further on, there was a man in sunglasses and a woollen hat leaning on a drainpipe. He was wearing a heavy green coat and had a mottled skin and an untidy beard. He smelled like the old haystacks at the bottom of her mother's garden, and…she couldn't place it for a moment, but then she got it. The man smelled like her father's bedroom when Céline had been there all night.

Even though there was a good breeze Laura wished there was a window she could open to blow away the smell of the man more quickly. She felt him watching her through his dark glasses.

She waited until she was well past before beginning the careful process of removing her chocolate flake.

'Mmm…' she murmured.

When the chocolate was finished Laura had noticed that the street around her was less crowded. She took a turning rising steeply away from the main road thinking that it might give a view to the jetty where the cruise ship was berthed.

There were no more strings of bunting between the grey stepped roofs, no gay yellow, red and blue flags that flickered like snakes tongues tasting the wind. There were still kerbstones to balance on.

There were some nasturtiums growing through black railings around a window that sunk gradually lower and lower as the slope cut across the ground floor of the house. If her hands had not been occupied she would have picked a flower to eat.

After this, there was a break in the line of houses, a tarmac driveway with bushes along one side. At the end was a kissing gate and a larger metal gate for vehicles. There was a sign with a dog crossed through in red. Beyond was a flat green open space. Laura walked towards it.

She shimmied around the gate careful not to disturb the hinges. Taking a few steps forward she found herself by a perfect square of lawn patterned like tartan cloth.

Benches were arranged in pairs on each of the four sides. She took her place on one. She sat nibbling her wafer cone swinging her legs. What a funny place, she thought. It must have taken a lot of effort to make it flat.

She tipped her head backwards. A cloud performed the quick trick of turning from dog to dragon to elephant then, as if she and the water vapour were of one mind, it had become so nebulous and relaxed that it resembled nothing at all.

Thwack-thwack! Thwack-thwack!

The sudden disturbance jolted her upright. Her blood galloped around her veins.

The kissing gate was swinging shut behind the man in dark glasses. He looked over at her then shambled over to a bench outside the little clubhouse. It was the place most in the sun and most out of the wind. He'd sat in the centre then lifted his legs, twisted sideways and lay on his back, hands folded across his chest.

It had been then that she'd imagined a voice calling her name.

'Laura, Laura!'

But everything was peaceful at the square of grass.

Nobody might come here all day she thought. And she thought of her father and how much she loved him. And she thought of Céline and how boring she was. And she thought: what would they do if I were not there? Without me, wouldn't they find it quiet?

Father might realize Céline has nothing to say.

She pushed down with her hands, hovering above the seat and leaving sticky fingerprints on the bench. How did they get the grass so perfect? What were the rules for bowling? She stood up and stepped towards the metal edge separating the normal grass from the perfect grass.

The man was asleep on the bench. She was sure.

She rocked backwards then ran, marvelling in the plush velvety greenness that seemed to spring her upwards, running freely until she was at the centre. Then one, two, three, four… round and round spinning, arms out, arms in, arms high, arms low, until the green square tilted and tipped her over onto her knees.

Laura breathed deeply then pushed up on to her feet. She skipped along the diagonal and off the perfect grass, passing within a few feet of the sleeping man. Without stopping she blew him a kiss.

She zigzagged through the gate letting it thwack closed behind her then she'd gathered pace and raced past the nasturtiums. She'd taken the steep turn into the main street leaning inwards and kept going at full pelt until too many people finally impeded her way.

She'd reached the giant's ice cream, un-melting under the high sun.

She skipped along the river of stone, now wending gently back, her breath returning evenly. She'd passed the scaffolding. She walked past the clothing shop, past a girl playing the violin like she wanted it to catch on fire.

Next there was a souvenir shop with carousels filled with postcards of stone ruins and puffins. Laura had reached out and taken one of the bird. She slipped it quickly into her pocket. She would send it to Sandrine – who she loved and missed, who had once said to Laura that Céline was jealous of her.

Further down the street, where the slabs petered out and were replaced by proper road, she saw Céline sitting at an outside table of a small café.

Céline had her coat collar turned up and a handful of shopping bags arranged around her feet. She was reclining with a cigarette in hand.

'Hello,' said Laura.

'You had better tell your father what you want,' Céline said. 'He's inside.'

Pierre appeared in the doorway. He had smiled at Laura.

'Chips?' he said.

'No,' said Laura. 'Soup – as long as it isn't cauliflower. And hot chocolate with marshmallows.'

'Okay.'

Laura sat down opposite Céline to wait for her food.

She remembered clearly the way Pierre had smiled because he wore the expression so infrequently. She had thought he couldn't possibly know what she had been doing. No one could.

Now, on the bus Laura suddenly believed differently. Her grin slipped. She felt an unexpected prickle of tears.

Pierre's earphones still hovered in mid-air. He spoke again.

'I noticed,' he said. 'I noticed that you were gone.'

For a moment she felt as though all her thoughts were completely transparent, everything, her whole life was laid open.

'You?' she said.

'I didn't need to come and find you, did I?'

'No,' she said. 'I was just fine.' Laura paused, then added, 'Thank you.'

She was blushing when the bus jerked forward, toppling her sideways.

Balance

He was not a whimsical man, no one who knew him would describe him as such, yet he was struck how the fallen flowers of the overgrown rhododendron looked like upturned bonnets abandoned by miniature imps. It reminded him of his daughter – she would probably have picked one up and carried it with her.

It was the second time he had thought of her that morning. The first had been more painful, slicing through time in the way memories did, evoking the old familiar doubts. The events and emotions of a day in summer many decades ago that had piled-up one on top of the other, then condensed into a moment of sharp anguish.

The pricking pain faded. He'd recovered his self-assurance even before the girl who'd caused the sensation crossed the road. She had been balancing on the kerbstones, avoiding the cracks between the thin rectangles of concrete. She balanced without really concentrating, keeping one eye on an ice cream and now and then looking up at the bunting strung between the tops of buildings along the narrow street. The dark-haired girl wobbled, she bent at the hips and swayed to avoid stepping down into the gutter, her ice cream pirouetting in the air. Without losing balance she corrected her position, licked around her cone then carried on.

She caught his eye as she flicked her head right and left before stepping into the road. He couldn't read the expression on her face; he never had much empathy with that age and sex – not even with his own daughter. The girl looked away quickly. Her dark ponytail, disarrayed by the breeze, swung behind her as she disappeared around the corner away from the parade of shops.

The girl had already gone when he passed the turning to the bowls club on the way home, like she had vanished into thin air.

He made an effort to keep his steps measured and firm, the

heel connecting firmly with the ground and the foot rolling onto its big toe. It was an old habit; a technique that encouraged his state of mind to steady and to match his outward appearance.

His trimmed moustache and precisely combed hair had not changed in style since he was a young man. A black and white photograph taken in the first week of his employment was still a fair representation of how he looked now, although the colour of his hair had altered.

His appearance had been considered old fashioned even then: the lean face with small intense brown eyes, framed by lids that drooped ever so slightly at the corners, and a thin mouth partially obscured by hair that was parted symmetrically on his upper lip.

The few photographs he possessed of himself before this time presented images that were foreign to him. He had clear unblemished skin, a broad smile and unruly tufts of hair. He had no idea what he had been thinking as he posed. Examining them, as he had done recently, only made his childhood feel even more lost to him. It seemed to have passed too quickly for him to remember, in an orgy of frenetic activity that had one day delivered him up as a young man. It had left him unable to imagine what it was like to be a child, and even with his great intelligence, unable to predict what a child might do.

His wife had admired his quick wit and the way he toyed with words to amuse people. Before they met, at the age of eighteen, he had already perfected raising his left eyebrow to throw into question the most earnestly developed arguments of his school friends. To his father's lasting distaste he had built a career out of the re-interpretation of words and had become a lawyer, principally involved in lengthy commercial matters. It was the wrong type of success for a man whose vicarage walls bore nothing except selected quotes from approved translations of the Old and New Testament. His mother, whose memory was also confined to his childhood, had died from pneumonia, choking for nights on end while his father sat vigil in the church next door.

He supposed that had she lived longer his history might also have been different. It was the shuddering discomfort he experienced in the presence of his mother-in-law which had led to him becoming, for the first time in his life, solely responsible for his daughter. It was more acceptable that he used some of the many days of holiday he had accrued to look after his daughter Sarah while his wife was in hospital for the delivery of their second child than permit his mother-in-law to become resident in their house.

At seven years old he did not expect Sarah to be awkward about what she ate or distressed by the absence of her mother for a week. He planned that they would take strolls in the garden, browse books from his library and if the weather was fine explore along the cliffs. They walked side by side leaving the hospital. He answered succinctly, and as anatomically correctly as he was aware, the questions regarding birth that she asked him.

Later, as they climbed the steps into the entrance hall of the house it struck him, for the first time, that the sole indication that a child inhabited the place was Sarah's bodily presence. Her noise, movement and possessions were limited to distant upper spheres of the house, where he rarely went. In the dark wood-panelled hall, with its old-fashioned hat stand, semicircular gate-leg table and smoke tinted mirror, she glowed white and small, moving fleetingly from foot to foot.

He remembered clearly how she'd hopped along the diagonal lines of black tiles on the geometric floor pattern, and the way her dress lit the way before him down the corridor.

They ate scrambled eggs for breakfast the morning before it happened. Although they had prepared them together in the kitchen he insisted they were deposited in the house dumb waiter and taken up to the dining room to be eaten. They ate their meal seated opposite each other on the smooth walnut table beneath the heraldic carvings on the ceiling and watched by the petrified unicorns that supported the fire grate.

There was still no news from the hospital. The previous day had been spent satisfactorily examining and cleaning the contents of the large bell jar in the study. There were five taxidermied blue tits in various naturalistic poses arranged amongst a background of dried flowers. He had explained the basics of preserving and mounting animals and the usefulness and aesthetic value of a well-posed bird, while she nimbly removed dust from their wings.

He had decided that this was going to be a more active day and they would need to be properly fortified. The eggs were soft and perhaps a little watery, but nothing was left on their plates at the end of breakfast.

Sarah had chosen to wear her first communion dress that morning. He saw no reason to prevent this, but also required she put on walking boots before they set out.

The wind raised goosebumps beneath his shirt sleeves even though the fresh blue of the sky and companionable sunshine proclaimed spring had long since arrived and that summer was close at hand.

The botany he recalled from his youth was easily capable of answering Sarah's questions about the things they passed as they walked through the wilderness outside the garden wall.

'Can I swing on this branch?' she'd asked, curling her fingers around a low bow.

'I'm sure you can, if you put your mind to it,' he'd answered, without slackening his pace. Without his assistance he knew she would fail and soon be catching him up.

Soon they left the safety of the wood. He noticed wet mud had flicked onto the hem of her dress as she walked before him through the overgrown footpath towards the cliff top. After a few hundred yards there was a short sharp transition from being surrounded by the protective growth of willow, elder and nettles to being exposed and rudely protruding into the air. The wind whipped the breath from the cavity of his mouth and rippled the ankle high tufts of coarse grass.

Sarah stopped and waited briefly where the sky opened up, before fluttering away, like a piece of paper dancing on the wind.

She was ahead of him and in the open. He remembered a brief, pure burst of pleasure seeing the thrill the speed her own momentum gave her as she raced downhill to where the path joined the cliff top walk. Again she waited for him, crouched in a hollow out of the wind, peeling apart the thick stems of the grasses, her skirts tucked beneath her knees.

They continued to the very edge of the land. The breeze was sharper and less tempered by the sunshine. Although she never complained about the cold she must have felt its chill.

Something about the strength and energy of the wind seemed to infect her. Her running became more vigorous and spirited. She was often out of his sight. It touched him too, this raw force of the air and the high outsideness of it all.

The last time she ran back to find him she asked him something. Her eyes flashed, reflecting the sun above. The words of her request were stolen by the curling, grabbing wind. Without thinking he'd nodded in reply and she slipped away, her hair swinging loosely around her shoulders.

The rise of a small hill obscured where she had gone. Half a dozen steps later he saw her. He couldn't grasp what he was seeing at first. The dark leather of her boots and the fluttering flag of her white dress gave the impression that she was floating. She was too high up for the image to make sense, until he made out the black vertical iron bars of the railings against the deep blue of the water. She balanced on an inch of steel, arms outstretched for balance, nose and chin tipped downwards, eyes fixed on the rail in front of her.

He found he could not move, while every blade of grass bent and bowed towards her, while her hair lifted and fell like she was a goddess of the air. He watched her left leg move through the arc of its step. In his mind's eye he saw her miss the foothold she sought.

At last he understood the content of her wind-stolen request.

He began to sweat. The bitter taste of panic rose in his throat. He felt such a weeping sense of failure and regret, such helpless anger.

The memory of the fear always came back to him like that.

But no, it hadn't ended like that. Sarah had come down when he'd called. She had promised never to do it again and they had walked back to the house together. The next day the baby had been born. A week later he had gone back to work, and they went on living as they always had done – soon everyone became used to his white hair.

It had all been so long ago. It was just one silly little moment, so long ago.

Carer

Angelique squinted at the weak orange sun low under the branches of the big tree and wiped the condensation from the window with her palm.

'Some sunshine t'is mornin',' she said, patting her wet hand on the folds of her skirt. Then she announced, 'I want to go to the market. Get something special for us to eat.'

Aubrey slurped the hot tea over his gums. He watched the uneven roll of her figure moving around to the side of the bed. She began to untuck his sheets.

'It's sure cold though, and frost on the windscreens. Time to get out your wool,' she said.

She searched around in the wardrobe then moved on to the drawers. She clicked her tongue as she pulled out his old grey cardigan with leather buttons.

'We need to take you shopping.'

'Eh?'

'Take you shopping, Aubrey. Get you something warmer.'

'Money's in the drawer.'

He pointed to the bedside table. Angelique nodded and smiled. She knew there wasn't much there.

'Might be something in the market if we're lucky,' she said. 'Now put your tea down.' She started unbuttoning his shirt. 'Those are nice dresses,' she commented as she untucked the cloth from around his waist, 'nice and colourful.'

'Dresses?'

'Hanging up,' she said. 'Your wife's they must have been.'

His faded grey eyes searched back through time trying to remember the owner of the garments hanging in the closet.

'She's dead,' he said, 'take them away. You take them if you want. I don't know why they're still here.'

'Too small for me,' laughed Angelique, moving to the wardrobe. 'But the shawls might help keep the cold out.'

She touched a soft square of fabric with the pink ends of her

127

fingertips.

'Take them,' he said.

Angelique admired the detail of the roses on the black background. Even though she didn't usually wear black – it never looked right against her skin – she decided to wear the shawl for the walk to the centre of town. Everything else she put into a black bin bag and onto back seat of the car to sort through later. There were other shoes and scarves she might use. Something might fit her sister, although since arriving in England she'd also started to grow fat.

Aubrey leaned on her arm. His gaze drifted from the emptying branches of the hedges to the cars turning quickly out of the one-way system into the backstreets. His hands were cold; even with gloves on they always were.

'Where are we going?'

'The market,' she told him. Then she said, 'Nowhere sells real good fresh fish here, but that man's as good as it gets.'

By the time they reached the crossing outside the post office the temperature had risen enough for their breath to disappear easily in the air. The lights were already back to green by the time they were half way across. Angelique encouraged Aubrey onto the pavement, keeping the traffic stopped with her eyes.

'Did you want to rest, Aubrey?'

He didn't respond. She raised her voice.

'Sit down here. You have a prescription. I'll go in the chemist.'

'I do? Thank you. I'd like a sit down.'

She was back ten minutes later with her nails freshly painted from the cosmetics aisle tester pots.

'You look after me so well, Angie,' he said as they moved off.

After a few steps he cleared his throat into a square of cotton handkerchief and pushed it into his pocket.

'Are we finished now?'

'We're going to the market,' she laughed. 'You can't remember anything can you?'

She laughed again good naturedly, while Aubrey shook his head.

'I don't suppose I can,' he replied. 'I'm such a nuisance.'

'Don't worry. We're never bored are we, Aubrey?'

He liked her smile. It was broad and white against her dark

skin. He might even have considered her pretty if she had long hair. It was cut so short it was hardly like normal hair – more like wool he thought some days.

He liked it that she wore bright colours. Today she wore a bright orange shirt tucked into a brightly patterned skirt that swished around his legs. As they walked together he noticed the painted toenails peeping out of her sandals. She always wore sandals no matter how cold it was.

He used to like the market. When he was a boy the fruit and veg man would let him take an apple and there had been giant gobstoppers on the sweet stall. There were no electricals for sale then just food and things for the home, proper mops made of string and brushes made of two parts. You could take anything back if it broke.

'Make some room, make some room.' Angie clicked at anyone who got in his path. 'Mind out the way.'

Whenever they stopped she created a space for him to stand next to her.

He let her look after the money. He didn't like to carry it around with him any more. The coins made his wallet feel heavy and the notes seemed to change so often he couldn't tell if he was being fiddled when he handed them over.

'Nice and snug. Easy to get on as well. Keep your hands nice an' warm in those pockets. Eh, Aubrey?'

He nodded.

The fabric was light and warm – not wool though. The colour was green, armyish he thought, with purple patches here and there.

'Much better,' she said. 'Wash over and over these do, not like wool. None of that rinsing and hand washin'.'

He felt cold when he took it off to be put in the stripy bag.

The awnings and shelters of the stalls cast cold shadows around them. He didn't recognise the fishmonger in his wagon or the name of the fish that Angelique asked to be weighed out.

'I'll make you Ndolé,' she told him, dropping the wet package into her bag. 'Don't worry, you've had it before. It's stew with shrimps and greens and peanut butter. What a face you're making!' she laughed. 'You liked it. Ate up every bit.'

A hearty 'Heh, heh, heh,' came out of her mouth and her

eyes half closed.

The queue of cars waiting to leave the car park slowed their progress away from the stalls. His knees ached from standing up for so long and his lungs felt tight from the cold air. What he needed was a puff of tobacco to keep him going.

Angie wouldn't allow it.

'Not in my company, Aubrey. I don't want to lose my job because you get some kind of damned lung cancer. Keep yourself goin' and I'll make you a cup of dynamite when we get back. Lean on me. I may wobble but I'm not going to fall over.'

She barely noticed the increased pressure on her arm. Angelique wondered how much Aubrey weighed. She was sure his face was getting thinner. It made the remaining sprouts of grey hair around his ears and the back of his neck stick out more. Perhaps her sister could give him a haircut, she wasn't bad with a pair of scissors – and she needed the money. She always needed money. It slipped off her like the silk dresses they wore when they were little girls in the big government house back in Cameroon.

They walked slowly. The woollen scarf kept warmth next to her skin, its fibres began to tickle and itch around her neck. A smell of musty perfume released from the fabric. Angelique wondered if it made Aubrey remember his dead wife.

Next to her, Aubrey was trying to hum something as he walked. She didn't know the tune. His breathing was laboured.

'Nearly there, Aubrey. I'll go ahead and open the door.'

It was an unpleasant surprise to find the deadlock already unbolted.

She recognised the shadow falling through the kitchen door. She controlled her breath by releasing it slowly through her nostrils. He must have noticed her reaction.

'Is it your boy?' asked Aubrey.

'No, he's in school today,' she replied.

She held out her arm to steady him over the lip of the double glazed door. Aubrey raised his hand to hold the banister while she eased the coat from his shoulders and loosened her scarf.

'Hello, who is it?' Aubrey called.

A man appeared through the doorframe holding a mug in one hand and a cigarette in the other. He looked at them critically without smiling. There was the stale sharp smell of instant coffee.

'Where've you been?' he said.

'Where have we been?' Aubrey repeated to Angelique.

'To the market. You chose a nice new jacket to keep you warm. It was green.'

'Oh, yes. Do I owe you something for it?'

'It's all sorted,' she replied.

She glanced towards the man who'd entered the house while they were out. His gaze lingered on the roses around her shoulders and he lifted a cigarette to his lips.

Aubrey turned his attention more closely to the man in the doorway.

'You seem to know your way around,' he said cheerfully, gesturing with an unsteady finger at the cup of coffee.

Angelique cut in before Aubrey could say anything else.

'And I promised you a cup,' she said, folding away the scarf and arranging their shopping behind her on the doormat. The rustle of plastic bags was followed by the swish of her skirt. 'Let's get you sitting down, give them old bones a rest.' As she guided Aubrey to the living room she turned back and said, 'No smoking inside. Same rules for you as your father.'

He raised the cigarette and sucked. The tip glowed red.

'More shopping?' he called from behind her. 'What did he need this time?'

She ignored his question and concentrated on Aubrey. She positioned him by a chair in the living room. He bent his legs slightly and leaned backwards and settled into a carefully arranged pile of cushions. When Aubrey was comfortable she left him and returned to where his son leaned against the kitchen units. She would make proper coffee, boiling the grounds on the stove. She never touched the freeze-dried rubbish kept on the counter.

'What d'you want, Sid?' she said.

'Can't I come round once in a while to see how the old man's doing?'

'He's fine, just confused now and then. He's an old man. It'll happen to you one day. Go take that smoke outside.'

He took two steps, opened the back door and flicked the

butt into the clover-invaded grass.

'You're a real bitch, Angie. Won't even let him have his smokes.'

She didn't look up as he walked past.

She scraped a spoon over the pan bottom to stop the grinds burning. On the next ring the milk hissed as bubbles burst against the hot sides of the pan. She heard voices in the sitting room, one low and uncertain and the other assertive and repetitive. She rubbed her hip, easing the ache of an old injury worsened by the cold.

She tipped the black liquid slowly, resting the spoon on the lip to catch any grinds floating on the surface. The smell wrapped around her like a blanket. She felt for a moment like she was back in her grandmother's kitchen, surrounded by warm air and pestered by fat lazy flies. It reminded her of all the cousins and aunts and uncles she'd not seen for years. It reminded her of afternoons spent braiding little Diane's hair when she'd lived in France.

For all the sadness of moving on again, even with the cold, it was better to be here and working. She made her coffee darker than Aubrey's then stirred two spoons of sugar into each.

Aubrey looked up and smiled when she came through. Angelique positioned a table by his elbow and placed his cup on a woven mat.

'Angie, this is my son,' he said.

'I know,' she replied.

'Have we been out this morning? He says the house was empty.'

'Dear, dear, you'll forget your head tomorrow,' said Angelique. 'We've been to the market.'

'Oh, yes, that's it – the fish van. She's making me en-do-lay for dinner. Did I say it right, Angie?'

She smiled and nodded. He caught her by surprise sometimes remembering things like that. Sid stared at the clock on the mantelpiece, like he wished the glass would crack.

They sat in silence apart from the soft tick-tock.

'I was telling Dad that you shouldn't be using any of mum's things,' said Sid.

'He wanted to give them away,' she replied. 'He's got no use for them.'

'What's he talking about, Angie? What things? Did I do something silly?'

She shook her head.

Aubrey looked around the room, his eyes seeking familiar objects; his fingers searched for each other and quietened themselves on his lap.

'You keep giving things away, Dad. I might want something you know.'

'Might you?' Aubrey said. 'What do you want? I don't need anything do I, Angie?'

'You don't need her permission,' said Sid.

'What does he want?'

'I don't know, Aubrey. Drink your coffee.'

'What do you want?' Aubrey repeated, his hands flapped but did not move from his lap.

Angelique kept her eyes on Aubrey. Refusing to give Sid the satisfaction of having her attention. What *did* he want? There was nothing left of value in the house.

'She's taking it all,' said Sid. His voice was proud with bitterness. 'Bit by bit. She's taking it. She gets paid you know, for every minute she claims she's here. She takes advantage of you, Dad.' Sid turned to Angelique. 'He doesn't *need* any more clothes.'

'Whatever you say,' she replied, stirring up the sweetness at the bottom of her cup.

'You look like I did at your age,' interrupted Aubrey.

'I'm not like you,' Sid replied tersely.

'No,' said Aubrey. There was a pause then he added, 'It's nice of you to come around.'

'I'll start making notes of what's missing,' said Sid, 'claim it back out of your wages.'

'You do whatever you like,' said Angelique.

Aubrey searched for his handkerchief in his pocket. He raised it to his lips and covered his mouth to cough.

'I'm sorry. Who did you say you were? This is Angie. She comes in to make sure I get up in the morning.'

Angelique smiled. Aubrey always remembered her name.

'Jesus, I can't stand it! You'd drive anyone nuts.' He stood up and paced up and down in front of the blocked up hearth. 'You…you…'

'Is there a problem? Did I do something silly?'

Angelique let the grains slide down to the bottom of her empty cup. Her grandmother had taught her how to read those as well.

'Just so you both know, I'm watching you from now on.'

Sid headed for the door. She stared straight ahead at Aubrey. There was the poor slam of the plastic double-glazed door and he was gone

She let the silence fall then said, 'No Aubrey, you did nothing wrong, nothing at all. He'll not care to bother us too many times, not while I'm looking after you.'

Carpe Diem

Wells ran his fingers over where he'd sliced into the rope. Down below, Akram and Stevens were throwing sweets in the air. Mostly they were unsuccessful at catching them in their mouths, they cracked off their teeth and bounced down the slope into the gully.

'Done it yet?' called Stevens.

'Yeah, seems fine.'

Wells descended the beech tree. Momentarily concealed from view he patted the pocket that held his penknife.

There was the sound of a scuffle nearby.

'Push off, I'm first.'

Travelling in an up-swinging arc Akram sailed outwards until he was at least twenty-feet from the ground beneath.

'Waahooo!'

As he swung back Akram stretched out his foot, connected with the trunk and swung away again. The rope creaked.

'My turn,' said Stevens, reaching forward to catch the rope.

Wells climbed down the last of the trunk, his hiking boot flattening a young bracken growing through the roots of the overhanging tree. He sat down and watched the swinging rope.

Last year he'd lost his footing in the gully. His feet had skidded in the leaf litter and become tangled with a hidden root. He'd overbalanced and as his body slid downwards his right foot remained caught fast in the root, bent backwards and unnaturally flat. As the ankle joint strained Wells had tried to take his weight on his arms, but it was impossible to get purchase on the dusty slope. He panicked and screamed.

Afterwards his classmates claimed they thought he was joking. Stevens, who had been closest, said he couldn't see that Wells's foot was tangled. Akram had told Ms Standwell he thought Wells was faking to get out of finishing the walk. Even she had tried to convince him it was just a bad sprain on the drive to hospital.

The ankle had needed surgery twice. Wells was immobilised for eight weeks at home. His mother hadn't encouraged visitors. She'd removed the television from his room, collected schoolwork from his teachers and told him it was a chance to get ahead.

She'd taken time off work to stay at home with him. Even though she usually discouraged anything non-academic, she had accepted his target of participating in the Silver Award weekend – his mother liked awards.

She didn't know how much the ankle still hurt. He had learned who would sell him over the counter pain medication and to hide the continuing pain.

Ms Standwell had deliberately put him with Stevens and Akram, and told them to 'work as a team.' Now, here they were back at the gully.

Stevens wedged the knot between his legs, gripped the rope with both hands, and waddled as fast as he could to the edge. He was lighter than Akram. The tree shook less violently and he swung smoothly through the shade-cooled summer air.

When Stevens returned for the second time Akram leaned out and shoved him hard, sending him into a spin.

'Heh, heh. Try and get out of that!'

Akram flicked up a stone with his trainer then volleyed it towards the spinning boy.

'Shouldn't we try and get to checkpoint five?' said Wells. 'We could be back early.'

Akram ignored Wells's question, squinting into the woods on the other side of the gully.

A bright green beetle the size of a thumbnail pinged from somewhere onto Wells's knee. He flicked it away, regretting having said anything at all.

Stevens began counter-spinning and swinging back towards them. On his next return he made contact with the bank and dismounted from the rope. He was laughing, but somehow it sounded forced.

'How about you, Wells?'

'Nah.'

'What'd you bother checking the rope for?' said Akram.

Stevens held out the rope to Akram. He accepted it, lowered

his hand to the knot, then drew it behind his back with a straight arm and flung it forward. The knot swung bandily through the air then flicked back, forcing Wells to scramble to his feet.

'What you do that for?'

'Calm down, Wells,' said Akram. He mimicked his classmate's high voice. 'Let's get to the next checkpoint so Ms Standwell can get off early to the pub.'

'I didn't say that.'

'We finished the route last year remember. It's not going to be any effort. Make her wait.'

'You reckon?' said Stevens.

'All we're going to do when we get there is be stuck in a tent,' said Akram.

Wells looked up to where the rope looped over the limb of the beech tree. Stevens would do what Akram wanted; he didn't have any choice but to join in.

'What then?' said Wells.

'Might get served at the Red Lion?' suggested Stevens.

'Not with him,' said Akram, nodding towards Wells.

Wells bent down, slipped his fingers down the inside of his sock and scratched his scars. They were hot and sore.

Akram turned anti-clockwise. He pointed to a broad path leading away from the gully. Nailed to a tree about six feet above the ground was a sign saying, 'PRIVATE PROPERTY, NO TRESPASSERS.'

'Let's try this way.'

'Brilliant,' said Wells, 'trespassing on private property. Epic new idea.'

Stevens remained where he was, flicking an old baggage-handling tag attached to the top of his rucksack.

'Come on,' said Akram. He picked up his pack then glanced over at Stevens and added, 'I've got some booze.'

Stevens swung up his bag and began following Akram.

Wells stood up. He adjusted his shoulder straps and after a brief look back at the gully walked towards the path. His painkillers were wearing off. He felt seedy, caught between enjoying and hating the novelty of being outside. The glow of the sky blurred pink and green through the shifting branches.

The track ran parallel with the bottom of the gully, separated from it by an increasingly broad bank. Overhead, pale branches of young beeches clashed with the limbs of crooked oaks.

At checkpoint four they'd had a clear view of the South Downs. Ms Standwell had been waiting for them on a campstool reading a book. She suppressed a yawn while marking-off their names. If she had known them better she wouldn't have thought it a good idea to put them in a team. Wells caught sight of the cover of her book. It was a well-researched historical fiction; utterly predictable. Ms Standwell was predictable; hysterical if a class played up, but easily mollified by a half-decent piece of Latin translation and if *anyone* showed an interest in Greek she was all over them like a rash. Wells found it embarrassing, but he'd observed that Stevens and some of the other boys liked it. He wondered if it was because he was younger than the rest that he didn't understand.

Akram walked in front, his stride an exaggerated swagger, hips pushed forward almost comically by bulging thigh muscles. His hand grabbed at the top of ferns, yanking them out of the soil. At school he ate, played sport and hit people over the head. His prodigious rugby ability made him exempt from academic pressure. Stevens, a few yards behind, sashayed by comparison.

Nothing except for a barbed-wire fence distinguished the track they were on from the forestry commission paths they had followed earlier in the day.

Akram punched Stevens lightly in the arm.

'Remember the time I jumped out of the window in French? Pullinger's such a dickhead.'

Stevens didn't reply.

'What d'you think, Wells? Pullinger's a tosser.'

'Whatever,' replied Wells.

Akram called louder – more expansively – into the woodland, 'Mr Pullinger's a tosser!' then after a pause he breathed in dramatically and proclaimed, 'Craig Wells is a tosser!'

He chuckled to himself and slashed at the ferns.

After they had walked on for a short way Stevens, who was a few paces in front, stopped.

'There's something over there,' he called back. 'Could be a house.'

Akram and Wells came to where he was standing.

'Where?'

'Come on,' said Akram.

He jogged ahead a short distance then split from the path. Stevens ambled to where Akram entered the woodland then followed. Wells hesitated; he felt for the knife in his pocket. He didn't like going off the path. It was their choice though, not his.

Somewhere out of sight Akram called, 'It's just a woodshed.'

Wells began making his way towards the voice. When he reached the small structure he immediately saw the axe leaning against its wooden boards. The head was solid-looking, the shaft had silvered to the same shade as the disorganised woodpile that Stevens was climbing. He waved his arms to keep his balance as logs slithered and rolled away.

On the open patch of ground between the woodshed and the log pile was a round cross-section of a tree trunk surrounded by splinters. Akram looked from the splitting-log to the axe. He shrugged off his bag, drew out a bottle and took a gulp. He replaced the lid then threw it to Stevens.

'Always fancied a go at this.'

'It's harder than it looks,' said Stevens swigging from the bottle.

'What'd you know?'

'We had a wood burner thing skiing last year.'

'D'you have a go?'

Stevens took another swig.

'A bit.'

'Come on then,' said Akram.

'Can't be bothered,' said Stevens.

He threw back the bottle. Akram caught it with one hand then strolled over to the axe. He weighed it in his hand, swinging it to and fro like an athlete warming-up to throw the hammer. He let the shaft slip through his hand and examined the blade.

'It's blunt.'

'Doesn't need to be sharp,' said Stevens, 'it's a wedge for splitting.'

Akram collected a log from the floor and placed it on the cutting round. He smirked in Wells's direction then swung the log-splitter. The blade wedged into the surface of the log.

'Told you it was blunt,' said Akram.

He pushed the log onto the ground, braced it against his foot and yanked out the embedded head.

Stevens half-slid, half-jogged down the woodpile. He took the log-splitter from Akram then selected a new log and placed it on the cutting round. With his left hand at the end of the handle and his right under the axe head he swung the log-splitter. He drew it in a large arc then brought it around and down sliding his hands together. The impact split the log into two almost even pieces.

'Whoa! Nice,' said Akram.

'Get one without knots in it,' said Stevens, handing back the axe.

Akram selected a new log and this time successfully split it in two.

Wells stood by the woodshed and watched.

Overhead the sound of aeroplanes was as constant here as over south London. They were always droning somewhere in the distance, fetching people hundreds of miles, all strapped in their cramped seats. His father had gone to France with his stepsisters Jeanie and Sophia. He sometimes saw them around, but they hardly knew each other. His mother kept it that way, that's how she wanted it. Sometimes, when Wells got really fed up with her, he felt like shouting, 'You're a f—ing control freak, that's why Dad left you!' But he knew he never would. It depressed him. Everything he did was under someone else's control.

He was so lost in thought he didn't notice how quiet the wood had become. As if the birds and insects had suddenly given up competing with the jet engines. It was so quiet he almost forgot anyone else was there.

'Your turn, Wells,' said Akram.

He held out the log-splitter.

'What? No.'

Akram raised his voice.

'Take it.'

'It's not hard,' said Stevens.

Wells was about to refuse again, but something changed his mind.

'Okay.'

His first attempt was unsuccessful; the second log nearly split cleanly.

It didn't take long for the game to start. Stevens had experience; Akram greater muscle; Wells more determination. To begin with successfully splitting a log in one strike earned a swig from the bottle.

Stevens split logs without trouble, as did Akram; Wells also had success. Splitting started to become straightforward. After his next go Wells decided to change things. Instead of relinquishing the log-splitter he picked up one of his fragments and replaced it on the cutting log. The others watched as he split it again. He picked up one of the smaller fragment and repeated the process. The new development of the game caught on. Stevens managed four consecutive splits, Akram only three.

'It fell over!' he insisted.

Wells reached to take the log-splitter. Akram held tight.

'Put it back up.'

Wells obeyed slowly and balanced the fragment of wood on its end.

'Now hold it,' said Akram.

'Hold it? You're kidding?'

'Come on, so it doesn't wobble.'

Wells placed his index finger on one side.

Akram pulled back the log-splitter then swung. Wells moved his finger away as the axe travelled through the peak of its arc. The log remained balanced and a second later was split into fragments.

'Nice one,' said Stevens.

Akram gave the log-splitter to Wells and took back the bottle from Stevens.

Wells selected a log and went to work. He concentrated hard, his back became wet with sweat, his hands hot from travelling up and down the wooden shaft. After four splits a section still remained intact that might be split again. He picked up the fragment from the ground and held it out to Akram.

'Hold it for me.'

'What? Get lost.'

Wells flipped the piece of wood. It spun in the air and landed back in his hand.

'I did it for you.'

Wells tossed the wood over to his classmate. It fell at Akram's feet. Stevens took the bottle thrust in his direction then shuffled backwards away from circle of splinters.

Akram picked up the wood, placed it on the cutting round and steadied it with his index finger. Wells drew back the log-splitter and swung hard.

He slid his hands with perfect timing. As the head swung down he felt sharp pleasure at the growing momentum. It was not a tool designed for cutting, but it was effective.

Wells smiled at the shock someone would get when they found the finger, and at the thought of Akram trying to conjugate Latin verbs.

Daisy Chains

The arrival of spring was never certain in my mind until I saw the first newborn lambs in the field rising up on the hill behind our house. The blunt grey outcrops of rock that had been barren all winter became first shelter for the expectant ewes escaping the southerly wind, and then a nursery for the skittish explorations of their offspring.

The spring before, when my mother had not been pregnant and I had still been six, I remembered her saying that the bleating of the lambs in the high pasture sounded to her like the cry of a baby when it had just been born, calling for its mother.

I watched her standing by the empty sink in our kitchen, arms folded over her tummy, staring at the top of the hill across the valley where the bad weather came from. In that rare moment of bodily stillness her eyes travelled backwards and forwards on the horizon. She was for an instant a mystery to me. I could never resist disturbing her and bringing her back to me with some question or request like: 'What can you see?' or 'Can I have a drink of water?' or 'Can we go pick flowers by the stream?'

As her tummy swelled in the winter of that year she had to stand further away from the sink as she cleaned dishes or sliced the meat and vegetables for our evening supper.

I had no interest in the arrival of the new baby. Christmas and my birthday and the presents they did or did not bring were my main concerns. Then one morning I stood on the cold lino of the kitchen and found Grandma stirring porridge on the stove. Her coat, bag and hat were neatly folded on one of the chairs around the table. She told me that my mother had gone down into town to the hospital during the night. I liked Grandma pretty much, but I didn't like porridge without any honey. When I asked she replied, 'No dear, you don't need it. I've made it with milk, it should be creamy enough.'

She had the same way of denying me small things that my mother did.

I ate the porridge quickly, hurrying the gluey mouthfuls, eager to leave Grandma behind and escape into the blue and green world outside.

Large drops of dew bent the tops of the newly sprouted grass that surrounded the house and the cold night had dampened down the scents of the honey flowers that spread around our driveway. By lunchtime their fragrance would attract the bees and fat dark flies would bother Grandma as she fried meat in the afternoon.

The absence of my parents from the house always excited me. I felt a tightening pleasure across my collarbone as I scuffed my feet towards the gate that led out to the road. There was nobody to witness my transgression of everyday laws. I didn't look for cars or really notice I had crossed the road until I was crouching down by the fence on the other side to get a better view into the field.

The ewe closest to me raised her head and took two paces backwards, forcing her suckling lambs to stagger and follow. They were the cutest things that I could imagine, in perfectly fitting white woollen jumpers, stretching their necks and twitching the flies from their ears as they fed. I shivered in the cotton dress I had chosen to wear.

'Here, lambies,' I called, pulling up some of the juicy clumps of grass on the verge to tempt them over. I wasn't sure if they ate grass yet, they were so small. I remember thinking they might prefer a saucer of milk from the kitchen.

I heard the footsteps on the tarmac behind me just as I was remembering that you feed lambs milk from bottles not saucers, like baby bottles, but much bigger.

'You're not allowed out of the gate,' said Grandma, in that plain way of hers she used for the first time I did something wrong, and for when she spoke to my father.

'I'm looking at the lambs,' I replied, unbending a little from my crouched position on the ground. 'I want one to look after.' I pointed to the group I had been watching and said, 'She has two lambs. I could have one of them.'

'You rear them by hand only if the mother dies,' said Grandma. 'It's a lot of bother for the farmer.' Grandma scrutinised the sheep more closely, narrowing her eyes.

'Sometimes you can persuade a ewe to feed a lamb that's not her own. If she's had a stillborn you skin the dead lamb and use it to disguise the orphan.'

I wasn't exactly sure what she meant, but the procedure sounded cruel and improbable.

'It wouldn't be a bother for me,' I said. 'I would enjoy looking after it.'

I looked up at her foreshortened face, her set back chin, angular nose and flat grey eyes.

'I told you, they're reared by hand only if the mother dies; even then they don't always bother,' she said.

The mother ewe had gone back to grazing the short new shoots and all I could see of her was the clotted dirty wool of her flanks. I wanted a lamb, one all to myself. She would follow me around the garden and I would feed her milk from those huge plastic bottles.

I stood up.

'I wish she was dead,' I said.

'Don't be such a silly girl,' said Grandma.

'But I do. I wish she would die. Then I could have a lamb,' I repeated.

I turned my gaze to the lamb on the left who seemed just a fraction more perfect than its twin.

'Well, she isn't going to.' This time Grandma's voice was edged with impatience. She took her hands from her apron pockets and quarter turned to look down the road to the north. 'Stay in the garden,' she said, dissatisfied with the quiet empty road.

She walked away without taking my hand and was already across the road before I followed her. I left the animals without giving them a second glance. Instead I kept my head down, examining the loose chips of asphalt that had escaped from the hard-pressed surface of the road.

There was nothing else to do for the rest of the morning except stay out of Grandma's way. I felt listless amongst the busy birds and insects around me. The bleating of lambs carried on the wind and invaded my ears as I played, sometimes sounding alarmingly near, sometimes baffled by the thickening hawthorn.

By afternoon Grandma had finished cleaning out the cupboards and was moving onto her secondary tasks of windowsills and mirrors.

By evening I was happy to see my father returning in the blue car. He was alone, without mother or the new baby. As his foot stepped onto the driveway I skipped over and blocked his way out of the car. I began searching his pockets and scanning the inside of the car for treats. There should have been something for me, some compensation. I'd heard about the arrival of new babies at school from Laura Lentier.

'I haven't got anything,' he said.

He stood upright, ignoring my pestering, and closed the door behind him. He walked to the house keeping his eyes fixed on the open back door then disappeared into the dark passageway beyond the kitchen.

I had never seen Grandma cry before and those secretive grey eyes that she shared with my mother still did not betray her.

The baby came home four days later. It was the same day I was dropped at the gate by Madame Beauchene, whose son Nico was in my class. She wore fashionable clothes and nail varnish and perfume. It was not a smell I knew or liked. She drove far more quickly than my mother on the winding road up from the town. I was glad to be out of the car.

Grandma heard me coming down the passageway.

'Would you like to hold her?' she asked when I reached the doorway.

My father, sitting on the sofa next to her, glanced up from his newspaper.

'No,' I said. 'Dad, can I go out and play?'

He nodded. I could tell that Grandma didn't want me to go, that I should stay and meet my new sister. And I should pat her dark hair (not like mine) and hold her tiny fingers. But I didn't want to. Grandma would have to look after her.

Instead I went outside in my cotton dress. The breeze was cool and I sat on the grass near the car on the driveway for shelter. My feet and hands grew cold until my fingers fumbled and refused to thread any more flowers. I put the daisy chains I made by my pillow with a picture of my mother. But I could not stay inside.

I stood at the gate to watch the lambs playing as the light began to fade, following their glowing whiteness skittering across the meadow. I heard their bleating cries carrying and echoing across the valley, and I heard the noise of the baby inside the house. How similar I thought, how similar the sounds are.

Leyla's Legacy

By the time Leyla changed her mind about dying it was too late. The coughing wouldn't stop. Warm air, rich in aromas, drifted from the mountainside, yet it felt like frost settling ever more deeply in her chest.

Inhaling vapours from mint tea made her a little more comfortable. While the glass cooled at her bedside she watched her daughter-in-law, Gharzal, washing clothes in the courtyard. The rhythm of the splash-slop of water and cloth lulled her. It was Gharzal who eventually replaced the tea by her side and later brought flatbread with spiced lamb.

Leyla raised her handkerchief, muffling the noise of her coughing so it did not disturb the men in the mehmankhana above. Her husband, Bahij, disliked the intrusion of domestic noise.

Seeing her granddaughter, Reyha, peeping around the door frame, Leyla screwed up her handkerchief and tucked it under her pillow. She beckoned for her to come closer. The girl pouted, then waddled forward, as if the world were a swaying ship. Reyha took after Gharzal; her small features clustered together prettily like a flower. She also demanded a great deal of attention.

'Come here, Granddaughter. Have some bread. I'll sing to you.'

Leyla clicked her tongue and Reyha climbed onto the mattress. They heard creaking as someone climbed the stairs above. Reyha lay down. Sucking the bread she listened to her grandmother's rasping song, fiddling with the frayed ends of the old woman's headscarf. The sun cast crosses onto the wall through the wooden lattice and they slept.

Gharzal woke them.

'There you are, Reyha. At least you have been quiet. Come on, leave your grandmother. She needs rest. Do you want the toilet, mother-in-law? I can take you now. The house is empty of guests.'

'No. Not now. I will manage.'

'Let me take you.'

'No, no. Go on with your work.'

As Reyha left, crumpled and hot from sleep, there was something about her that reminded Leyla of her youngest daughter, Lana; the one who should have been looking after her now.

Allah had blessed Lana with a great beauty, unmatched by anyone in their neighbourhood. Her hair had fluttered about her face like dark feathers; no one had a child with eyes as dark, skin as creamy. But what He had given with one hand He had taken with another. Whenever she suffered from illness it took weeks for her to be well. Her ears often dripped with brown fishy-smelling liquid.

Leyla let her stay at the breast far longer than her siblings, longer than anyone knew. Still she fell behind. When she died, at nearly three years old, she wasn't much bigger than her brother Wafiq had been when he took his first steps.

Bahij told her, '*"Truly to Allah we belong and truly to him we shall return".*'

Bahij was a devout man, and after she had born him two sons there was a period when he left her alone to sleep at night. Her place was with the children, not with him. Lana was conceived when Dildar, her second son, was five. The pregnancy was comfortable, but she knew her husband had passed her something from the discharge that leaked between her legs. Leyla passed a hand over her abdomen. There was still soreness below her navel, in her womb; it had grown over the years.

She had never wanted sex with him. Whatever it was other wives hinted at, nothing stirred in her during the grasping and thrusting. She bore the duty silently, crying when he left her. The pain could last for several days. When he made her do other things that would not bring a baby, with her mouth and hands, he would bring back a jar of honey from the bazaar the next day.

'*"Follow up a bad deed with a good deed to cancel it out"*,' he told her.

Leyla turned slowly onto her side and stared at the clay walls. There were footsteps again, thud, thud; heavy and old. Bahij was descending the stairs, but he did not come to see her.

She thought about the wall. It had seen her children brought into the world. It had witnessed Bahij holding her up and hitting her with his belt, when she was too exhausted to stand.

He had caught her taking a morsel of lamb, salty fat crisp from roasting, and giving it to Lana, before bringing the dish to where the men were waiting to eat. Her brother, cousin, Bahij's brother, brother-in-law and the shopkeeper Mahmoud were guests. Bahij beat her, then went back to eat. When the meal was finished he beat her again and had sex with her.

'*"Fear Allah and treat all your children fairly",*' he told her.

She had brushed the blood from the floor and washed the walls repeating, '*Make sure your food is good, and you will be one whose prayers are answered.*'

The next day her sister-in-law Sidra bathed the wounds on her back.

'You were really very stupid,' she said. 'It is his right to do whatever he wants with you now.' The salted water stung as she pressed. 'I'll leave you to bathe yourself,' she said gesturing to Leyla's private parts. 'Remember the prophet Allah says, *"If anyone of you becomes angry, let him keep silent".*'

If Sidra had listened to her own advice she might still be alive. She had argued with her son Aamil about money after Leyla's brother had died. He'd accused Sidra of not showing proper mourning and his mother had been punished. Aamil had gone off the rails, he'd left town and travelled to France. Leyla had heard that he now had a wife and two children; a girl named Leyla, who she prayed for, and a boy called Younas.

Aamil returned once a year to visit the market. He paid trappers to collect geckos and snakes he could sell for high prices abroad. Leyla wondered how the animals stayed alive – it seemed so unlikely they could journey so far and survive.

Leyla closed her eyes. '*Remember death when you are praying.*'

She could hear Gharzal scolding Reyha for pulling down the clothes hung up to dry. From the footsteps and voices in the mehmankhana above she knew Bahij was entertaining their unmarried son Dildar and his friend Malik.

Her elder daughter Eshal and her son-in-law Mahfuz arrived. Mahfuz ascended the steps to join the men while Eshal came and sat at her mother's side. Leyla pretended to be asleep.

'Mother? You were coughing in your sleep. Take some tea.'

Leyla sipped a little from the glass. The liquid was tasteless.

'Gharzal says you have not been to the toilet.'

'Why does she fuss? I'm old. I'm dying. I don't want to go all the way up there.'

'Then let me bring you a basin.'

'No. Tell me, where is little Nuzhat? I could do with her cheerfulness.'

Eshal fussed with her scarf.

'She is with Mahfuz's sister. I came to see you.'

'How does your sister-in-law treat you?'

'I think she is relieved Mahfuz is married, that I am there to share the work.'

'And Mahfuz? He is a good husband?'

'He is like Dildar,' Eshal replied.

Leyla looked for signs of disrespect in her daughter's face. There were none. It was a fact. Dildar was becoming middle-aged and showed little interest in marriage or a family.

'If it wasn't for his father I think Mahfuz would be happy not to have a son,' said Eshal. 'But he tries.'

Nuzhat was four years old, mischievous, exhausting and loveable. She would not welcome the arrival of a younger brother.

'Your cough is worse,' said Eshal. 'Your handkerchief is bloody.'

'I'm tired, I'm old. I have pain here, here, everywhere. Pass me some more tea and then I will sleep.' She held up her hand for the glass, but before she could take it doubled over coughing. Her stomach spasmed, forcing out a slimy vomit of bread and meat. Leyla lay limp.

'Lie back, let me tidy this.'

'Esha–'

'Shh.'

'*"Make the most of your youth before you grow old."*'

Eshal wiped her mother's lips and bathed her forehead.

151

'Nuzhat, can you bring her?'

'Perhaps tomorrow.'

'Who is that in the courtyard?'

'Gharzal singing. She should be here.'

'Shh. She is a daughter to me now you are gone.'

Another coughing attack began. When it finished Leyla was sweating from the convulsions.

'I will tell Gharzal to spend the night here with you. I will be back soon.'

Gharzal came later. Leyla heard her washing and Reyha splashing in the drain. Leyla remembered breaking the ice at the pump during winter and heating the water to make it bearable for the children to wash.

The noise of the street outside that had intrigued Leyla as a young wife no longer interested her. Bahij still loved the commerce of the district and inviting friends over during the afternoon to sip tea and talk. Fewer wives made the journey to the house. She could name four who had returned to Allah during the last five years.

Gharzal rolled out a sleeping mat and lay down with Reyha curled up on her breast.

By morning, the room was damp from dew drifting in from the courtyard. Leyla shifted her weight carefully, not wishing to disturb her daughter-in-law and granddaughter; aware that her need for the toilet would increase if she turned suddenly.

The cough started again, rattling at first, like poppy seed heads. Leyla swallowed hard. The urge came again. Tendrils stretched into her lungs, tickling and irritating, making her gag. She tried to clear the sticky mucus at the back of her mouth. The cough expanded upwards, boiling outwards, frothy; unstoppable.

Gharzal knelt over her.

'Sit. Lean on me mother-in-law. You must take something to drink.'

'No, no.'

'Your fever is back.'

'I must go to the toilet.'

'Now?'

Leyla nodded. The urge was painful and she was struggling

not to pass water.

'I can't take you upstairs. It's too early.'

'A pot?'

'I have one in the courtyard. Wait.'

Reyha turned over in her mother's blankets. She reached out her stubby fingers pressing them over Leyla's nose and mouth and babbling, 'Namnam, namnam.'

Gharzal returned quickly.

'You need to see Doctor Al-Jabbâr.'

'*"Truly to Allah we belong and truly to him we shall return"*,' answered Leyla.

Gharzal supported the old woman as she urinated. The pot filled with sour brown liquid.

'I had no doctor when my children were born. Bahij doesn't like the doctor,' said Leyla.

Reyha pushed against her grandmother.

'Reyha stop! Your grandmother is sick.'

Reyha leaned away. She twiddled a finger in her hair then headed towards the door.

'I have to light the fire.'

'Gharzal, do you know the saying, *"Remember death when you are praying"*?'

'I must go.'

Gharzal left. Leyla closed her eyes and listened to the sounds of the start of the day. Coughing burst out between her closed lips and through her nostrils, but she kept her eyes closed. Eventually she drifted back to sleep.

'Mother?'

Eshal was back, kneeling on the floor beside her.

'Has father been to see you? Let me speak to him.'

Leyla shook her head. What good was Bahij now? The thought was sudden, violent. Bahij with his thick waist and hard hands who rode her like a donkey when they were first married. 'Yah! Yah!' What good was he now?

The wind changed, smoke curled through the carved lattice from the courtyard.

'Mother, I have to go now. I shall speak to Wafiq.'

'No. He has his own worries.'

'Dildar?'

'What could he do? Go. Blessed be Allah.'

'Peace be upon him.'

Leyla held her breath as her daughter left. The next fit of coughing brought Gharzal from the courtyard. She knelt beside Leyla.

'Ssh, ssh. Try and rest.'

Dildar came. He leaned on the door frame looking down at his mother from above.

'What do you want, Dildar?' said Gharzal.

'I heard a noise.'

'Either bring Al-Jabbâr or go away.'

Dildar cleaned something from under his nails, separated himself from the door frame and slouched away upstairs.

'Go...' said Leyla. It was becoming harder to catch her breath, but she tried to make her voice firm. 'Go to your work. I'm not going anywhere.'

Later, at dusk, Reyha scrambled over her grandmother with careless poking limbs to lie beside her. Leyla dreamt of a banquet, richer than any she'd ever seen. She heard her daughter-in-law calling.

'Reyha! Reyha!'

Gharzal was in the dream with her, tiptoeing towards the endless platters.

'*Obey Allah and he will reward you*",' said a voice.

The calling was replaced by the sound of someone coughing.

Leyla opened her eyes. She saw Gharzal lift the hem of her scarf to wipe her lips. She noticed the dark patches under her daughter-in-law's eyes, and how slim her body had become beneath the folds of her clothes.

Reyha raised her arms up to her mother. With effort, Gharzal lifted her. The infant toyed with her mother's necklace, closed her eyes and rested against her mother. Then she drew breath, puffed her cheeks outwards, formed an 'o' with her lips and began to cough just like her mother had done.

Gharzal raised her hand to cover her daughter's lips. The sickness had spread. Leyla released her handkerchief, stretched out her fingers, and tried to speak. She swallowed hard, desperate to make her voice clear.

'Tell Bahij…Reyha…must see…Al-Jabbâr. Where is Eshal? …Where is Lana?…Where are my daughters? Gharzal…you are sick too. Do not be…find a new…you must never be silent.'

Gharzal kissed Reyha gently on the forehead. She took Leyla's hand, then closed her eyes and nodded.

Departures

I'm lying on the floor. No, not the floor – the ground. I'm lying on the ground, a stone wedged under my left buttock, hand in the dusty crease between car park and flowerbed, dust that's being picked up by the wind to knee-height, face-height, hem-of-cotton-skirt-height.

The woman's skirt blows aside as she crouches down.

'Are you all right? Can you hear me?'

She has just enough gap between her front incisors for it to be noticeable. I can hear her perfectly well.

The ground is warm, dusty and warm. Yellow-brown dust is sticking to my shirt. It has been washed and ironed, so the woman expecting me will see that I do have standards even living on my own.

'Did you trip? Can you tell me your name?'

She leans over me, places a hand on my forehead.

'It's okay,' she says to someone over her shoulder. 'Mummy's got to help this man.'

Her sunglasses have a dark tint at the top that fades on the way down. Her fingers are soft as she lays them on my neck.

'Can you move?'

The ground is warmer than my body, except for my hands; they have always been very warm. I've warmed plenty of hands, fingers frozen from weeding, rubbish bin emptying, shopping, carrying…

What a pleasant evening to be outside; rare, balmy. I didn't want to drive. Now I'm lying on my back, on the ground.

'Can you tell me your name?'

My name's never changed. Not like hers, the woman that's waiting for me. She has gone from Miss to Mrs, then to what? She could hardly go back to Miss again.

It took me by surprise when she said she liked the sound of being Mrs somebody again. Did she mean that she would like to marry someone else, or be married to me again? And which part of our past was it she thought was a mistake?

'Ambulance please,' says the woman in sunglasses. 'I'm outside the Lion's Yard, on the High Street. It's a man. Fifty I would say, perhaps a bit older. Actually, it's hard to tell. He's very suntanned.'

'Swarthy,' my ex-wife called me. She had been envious of my tanned skin. We'd lie with arms and legs tangled, like caramel and cream marbled together. She hated the smell of sun-protection cream and the way it laid greasily over her skin.

But rubbing it in had been romantic.

'Some on my shoulders...mmm...that's it. And my back. Did you do right at the base? I'll end up with red lines otherwise. Back of my legs as well.'

I remember the hotel room, some cheap package deal place with hundreds of balconies, walls painted green, long windowless corridors. She was wearing bikini bottoms, cool-skinned from the first shower of the day.

'That tickles,' she said.

'Tickles? Tickles here?'

'Yes.'

'I've never known anyone so ticklish.'

'You're taking a long time to rub it in...'

Later, she would complain about having to take another shower.

'How can I trust you after what happened last time?' she'd said, wagging the orange bottle at me.

'Didn't you en–'

'Try not to miss anywhere, that's all.'

She had stood in the doorway onto the balcony, wearing both pieces of her bikini this time, hair wet and unbrushed, tapping her foot. I applied blobs in a random fashion over her skin then began to slather and rub in the cream.

By the end of the week we were in strong disagreement over whether the sound of the air conditioning unit or the heat made it more difficult to sleep.

'I can't breathe it's so hot,' she said.

'Opening the window lets mosquitoes in.'

'There aren't any here. I'm not having that machine droning all night.'

'I heard one yesterday,' I said.

'The guidebook says there aren't any.'

'Well I heard one.'

She got up and opened the slide door.

'It's like being in an oven.'

I watched her shake ice out of a tray into a glass and go to sit on the balcony. I made my eyes into slits so I could observe her. I watched her sipping and swallowing, fidgeting the straps of her nightie. She sighed and looked over at me. Her gaze travelled deliberately along my body: toes, knees, thighs, groin, over my abdomen and chest to my face.

The expression on her face didn't alter. It struck me forcefully at the time how unmoved she was by what she saw. At the time it affected me.

I suppose it is because of the warm dust between my fingers that I recollect another holiday. There had been a light breeze, long sweeps of high white cloud in a cool blue sky. Claggy red cliffs rose unmajestically behind us, topped by a strip of grass, iron railings and a pavement leading to the outskirts of Paignton.

She was holding a wide-brimmed hat on her head as we sat on the beach. She experimented, moving her hand. The hat immediately lifted.

'You'll be holding it all day,' I said.

'So? Does it bother you?'

'It's the seaside. There's a sea breeze. You can have my cap if you like.'

'I don't want your cap,' she said.

My hair had started to thin a little on top. She'd rummaged in the straw basket at her feet then began to apply cream to her face.

'Rubbed in?'

'Mostly,' I said.

'Well? Where isn't it?'

'Here, and under your nose.'

I leaned forward to touch her face.

'I'll do it,' she said.

She didn't ask my opinion again.

'Where are they anyway?' I asked.

'Jill went to get a sun hat. Ronnie wanted a paper.'

'I think I'll pop back and see if I can get a book,' I said.

'Now? We've only just settled down.'

I stood up.

'Sure you don't want my cap?'

'No.'

I'd left her on the beach staring at the crashing waves. I could see that for a while they'd met each other's match.

Later, there were consequences.

'I'm furious with you,' she said. 'Completely furious. What the hell do you think you were doing? Where the hell were you?'

'It was Ronnie's idea. I thought you would have used common sense.'

'Common sense? What the hell do you mean by that!'

'That you wouldn't have sat there waiting.'

'You're calling me stupid now?'

'Come on. It must have been obvious.'

'You went to buy a bloody book. It started to rain, as it does here – quite often if you hadn't noticed. I didn't even have a coat. You had the car keys in your pocket.'

'Why didn't you walk back?'

'I was waiting for you! God, I'm so furious. I can hardly speak to you right now. So angry, that you could just go off like that.'

'Jill said she might go down to the beach,' I muttered.

'But she didn't. I was on my sodding own, all sodding morning, getting sodding wet. And there wasn't even sodding hot water when I got back to *this* sodding place.'

'That's not my fault.'

'You chose it. You said, "Let's have an English holiday for a change." It's rained every day; I've wrecked a pair of shoes and–'

'You can't blame me for the shoes,' I said.

'It's not about the shoes. God, you make me so angry. I can't even bear to be in the same room as you any more.'

She grabbed her wash bag from the chest of drawers, clasped it to her chest then swung around. She slammed the door of the bathroom behind her.

I heard the squeak of taps, the rush of running water. Through the rectangular pane of glass above the bathroom door I could see steam rising. 'If it's of any interest, I didn't have a very good round,' I called.

There hadn't been any reply.

In fact there hadn't been much conversation for the remaining three days of the holiday. I don't think our companions could have been unaware of our argument. They were after all staying in the room across the corridor in an establishment with only eight rooms.

When I appeared alone at breakfast the next morning Jill enquired discreetly if everything was quite well.

'Business as usual,' I replied, pouring cornflakes from a strange plastic container.

She had round eyes, not without some beauty. They had a very sympathetic look. I was surprised when she placed her hand on mine.

'Such a shame for you,' she said, and squeezed gently.

'He's having trouble breathing,' the lady in sunglasses says into her phone. 'No, I don't know him.'

She looks at me quizzically, leans forward and stares into my face. She's close enough for her breath to mingle with mine. It smells of mint.

'Do you have asthma?' she asks. 'No. I can't make out what he's saying. There's nobody with him.'

The moistness of her breath has a cooling effect. Ever so slight. I feel calm. Blackened cracked beams jut out under the roof above us. So massively over-engineered these Georgian buildings. Some of the timber was taken from ships, oaks felled to build the navy, brought back and hammered down, now the floor of a cheap solicitors office and the ceiling of an expensive picture framers.

'Yes. I can stay with him. How long will you be?' The woman looks at her watch then says, 'That's no problem.'

There's no more breath on my face.

My thoughts turn to my wife's withdrawal, first in one area, then another. Nothing melodramatic really, although there were accusations and undeniably there were faults. There were arguments, fighting talk, too much fighting in the end.

In the years after the divorce – well what didn't I do? I could do what I pleased. We never had children; perhaps we were

160

already too old for them, too set in our ways, too selfish perhaps?

I can feel the dust working into the weave of my shirt, into the creases of my trousers. It's like the dirt that builds up after weeks of travel – the sort of grime I had been ridding myself of in the shower before I left the house.

A two-week minibus tour of Slovenia – it was a grubby affair.

What were the chances my ex-wife would also be on it? Even though neither of us had moved far away from where we lived when we were married we hadn't seen each other for years.

When I first caught sight of her she was sitting on the back seat of the minibus wearing a straw hat, a mannish white shirt and a green scarf. We were the only English people on the tour, although everyone else understood enough to nod towards the points of interest mentioned by our idiosyncratic guide.

'This, you see this old woman, she's eating sausage, make her fat for winter. This, you see this new sports provision with AstroTurf and flooded lighting, this very good. This, this originally build three hundred and fifty years ago, destroyed completely and remade exactly the same. We stop here for unleaded petrol and…refreshments break. Toilet around sideways. Everyone get off now.'

The commentary was certainly less expert than promised by the colour supplement advert; even so we steadily followed the agreed itinerary.

There were fifteen people including our driver, our guide and our guide's stocky female companion. Her name was Anita and it seemed to be her job to go into restaurants to barter for evening meals. She sat next to the driver thumbing through gossip magazines emblazoned with photographs of over-fat and over-thin women wearing bikinis.

I owe Anita some gratitude; her methods of negotiation and her obsession with beauty magazines provided seeds for conversation with my ex-wife.

'Do you think the food cost less because it was lukewarm?'

'Possibly. What do you think of the house wine?' she countered. 'An acquired taste?'

Somewhere between mountain villages we lapsed into remembrances of bikinis and swimwear, and of the places we had visited together. There was one town in the foothills of the

Pyrenees we both remembered well. We had walked the thin streets, picking out fantasy investment opportunities from the narrow abandoned shops whose state of repair grew steadily worse as the eye travelled upwards. Inevitably there had been a hopeful immobilier placard leaning in the window. We'd joked that the town was an 'undiscovered tourist gem,' but really it was the kind of place that was unlikely to ever really change. Curiously we had both been more satisfied on our return than after visiting more exotic places.

In Slovenia we started flirting outside the concrete-floored, pipe-rusting, urine-smelling, water-dribbling toilets of petrol stations. We exchanged handfuls of bland crisps for explosively crumbly biscuits on the road; took our tea with lemon in the afternoon. Seats for dinner were prescribed by Anita; no one ever demurred. We were placed together.

'I had earwigs on my dressing table.'

'Perhaps they were friends with the woodlice in the skirting board?'

'Probably a raging social scene…'

'If you're an insect.'

'Slice of lemon?'

'If I must.'

'You're still on holiday.'

This morning there had been an awkward goodbye scene at the airport. My suitcase had come out on the carousel first. I hoicked it up, extended the handle then out of old habit stood waiting next to her. Someone bumped me on the shoulder forcing me towards her.

'Sorry. I didn't mean to–'

'Don't worry. It can't be long. I mean it's not like they could lose it or anything. You don't have to wait, really.'

'I suppose I don't.'

She turned to watch the bags shuffling past. Someone nudged me again.

'I'm sorry…' I said.

'I know it's very crow–'

'Actually, I wanted to say I'm sorry… about everything that

went on when we were married. I'm not sure I'd recommend the driver, or the guide, or the hotels to anyone, but you've been a first rate companion.'

She craned her neck and looked at me. She opened her mouth as if about to speak.

In that pose – with her lips parted, showing a glimpse of her teeth and tongue – I felt the strong urge to kiss her.

We had stood lip-locked, blocking the jaundiced post-holiday hoards from baggage carousel number seven. The tannoy announcement, the squeaky conveyor, the squawking, overtired, grumpy, travel weary crowd were gone. I felt for a moment that funny hurt-bliss of a teenage crush.

She must have felt it too.

We agreed to drive home separately then meet in the evening. It would also be sensible to shower and change, but of course unpacking could be left until later.

I knew walking would take a little longer, but then she'd promised we'd break into the duty free Bombay Sapphire. I also had romantic hopes.

I don't want to be lying here, on the ground in the dust. I have other hopes. I wanted to take her back to that curious little French town, to the cafe that overlooked the house with the lilac shutters.

An Informal Wake

'…three days, then next weekend I'll be back again.'

'Much to do?'

'No'

'Is it true? Did he leave it to that English woman, the one who bought the wreck on St Joseph and lives like a nun…?'

'…yes.'

'Don't you mind?'

'I was surprised. Who knows why he did it. He must have liked her. She came in a couple of times a week. Not the same as mother.'

'…well who could be?'

'Thank goodness.'

'You don't mean that.'

'You didn't live with her. Imagine if I'd brought Julia home.'

'It would have caused a stir.'

'And all the time your father wa–'

'We'll never know for sure.'

'But you have to admit…'

'Admit? Listen, no one was hurt but himself. He was just an old man who shouldn't have been fiddling around with a gun. Really, I should have taken the keys for the cabinet away.'

'You couldn't have known what he would do.'

'…well…'

'Try this. I think it's good.'

'Too good, slice it more thinly. There's plenty enough for the three of us. Here, take another.'

'The cheese?'

'It's young, fresh, if you li–'

'Do you think the bridge will fall down one day?'

'Not on us.'

'Why did they paint it blue?'

'Can't say.'

'It goes nowhere now.'

'No, it just doesn't go anywhere in particular.'

'What's the difference?'

'People go across, then they go where they like.'

'We're here.'

'I like detours…'

'At least the lamps will give us some light.'

'…I should have brought a blanket to sit on.'

'It's fine.'

'Can you see on the other side? Do you think he's watching us?'

'From up there?'

'… he's harmless. In fact, I think I'm getting to like him.'

'You're getting soft.'

'Where's the harm? There's something…I don't know…he's different.'

'At least it's cooler here.'

'Always is by the river.'

'The cemetery… that was hot.'

'Good God, wasn't it? All wearing black. Father Adibe was feeling it too.'

'You noticed?'

'…mopping his brow. Shall we open another?'

'Look, the light's gone off.'

'Must be bedtime…'

'You said your father asked for Father Bartholomew.'

'He did at the end, I don't know why, they couldn't have understood much each other said.'

'I always found him very consoling.'

'Consoling?'

'Anyway, he went back to England. I spoke to his housekeeper. I think that's who she was. Get this, she spoke French like a Parisian.'

'Really?'

'Hmm… She was very sympathetic. Anyway, he was busy. He had a meeting with his bishop.'

'We're all sympathetic you know.'

'He could have had another ten years.'

'I don't thi–'

'… look at Irma.'

'Oh, I forget you had her for lessons as well?'

'Didn't everyone? She had those delicious custard tarts. Just one mouthful.'

'… and the marzipan fruits…that sugar coating.'

'I always wanted to lick it off, but chomp-chomp…you had to eat it quick to get another.'

'… and keep your fingers clean.'

'You know, she predicted I would never marry…and that I would have, well look at me now.'

'You can hardly tell.'

'When's it due?'

'January.'

'What a month.'

'God, I know. I'll be big as a house. I know it.'

'Don't worry, I'll not be going anywhere.'

'What's your brother doing this year?'

'Pass me another. I don't know. He's infatuated with Céline.'

'At least that stage doesn't last.'

'…and Laura's not attached to her.'

'Poor thing, she was like a little ghost today, her face matched the gravestone.'

'It's how she always looks. Not a trace of colour. You wouldn't know it, but she does have some strange ideas.'

'What about the dog? Did you see it?'

'It's what they do now. They take it everywhere in that little bag.'

'…you have to feel sorry…'

'Of course…I didn't mind. There was no disrespect.'

'Would you like another?'

'No, it's the last. You have it – eating for two.'

'Don't remind me.'

'What's Gen's secret by the way? You looked after her boys didn't you?'

'…secret? I'm not sure what you mean.'

'Well… we're near enough the same age and I don't look like that.'

'She's always had money…her wardrobe…it's expensive and now she's stopped working.'

'…to look after the boys herself…'

'…no wonder she's more relaxed.'

'It's more. I swear it. Something's putting colour in her cheeks.'

'Well, I don't know …'

'Ask Irma. She knows everything.'

'No, no, no. She'd stop telling me anything.'

'Only half a glass remember.'

'What? You're not going to be fussy are you?'

'No. I just don't want…'

'…leave her alone. Anyway, did you get the changeover done? Beds made? Towels washed?'

'Yes, yes. Not much left behind except in the girls' bedroom. The usual magazines, money and crumpled up underwear and a handful of things that would shock their mother.'

'I thought they were nice girls?'

'They're teenagers…the mother's the problem. She makes herself unpopular. Can't see that she's no longer "Queen Bee," if you see what I mean.'

'Bees and honey?'

'Well, who can blame them for getting streetwise? Sorry, I don't mean that you made a mist–'

'Don't worry, I'm not offended. Of course I didn't plan…I don't mind. I'm happy about it really.'

'Happy?'

'I mean despite the funeral.'

'…I suppose, I'm happy too.'

'I'd go with that. More cheese? I can give you a hand tomorrow if Diane can tag along. Lend my expertise…'

'Yes, let me do something, too.'

'Okay. And will you be nice to Julia if I bring her next time?'

'Is she nice to you?'

'Very nice.'

'Then of course we will. We take all comers here. Now come on, eat something.'

Some Book Club Questions

1. Why does M. Lenoir try to kill himself? ('Brocante')

2. A brocante is a second hand market. What is the symbolism of the title in relation to the story?

3. Genevieve asks Theo, "I wonder though, what are you like underneath?" What is Theo like, underneath? ('Secret')

4. "Eugene thinks of saying, 'Do you realize that anyone who walks past knows you leave your daughter shut in that room, and have done since she was a baby? You should be ashamed.' But he does not." Why does he not? What would you do?

5. In 'Carer', does your sympathy lie with Angelique or Sid, Aubrey's son? Why?

6. 'Journey Back Home' is written in the first person, from Eddie's point of view; 'Carer' is written in the third person, from Angelique's perspective. Discuss in what ways these different styles affect your perception of both the stories and the vulnerable characters within them.

7. 'All this time and Marie didn't think Irma knew, but she did.' What do you think Irma knows? ('Irma Lagrasse').

8. What does Nico know? ('After the Afternoon').

9. What is Guillaume's attraction to women? ('After the Afternoon').

10. The collection finishes on a three way conversation after the funeral of M. Lenoir. Are you surprised by any of the secrets revealed in this final story? ('An Informal Wake').

11. Secrets and vengeance are two prevalent theme throughout the collection. Discuss some of the ramifications of secret keeping to characters such as Mary Ellen, Nico and Bartholomew. Is secrecy ever warranted and justifiable? What about vengeance? Do you think Barnby prevents the idea of revenge in a positive or negative light?

12. Consider the notion of guilt in the stories. How are characters affected by guilt in their lives? Are they justifiably filled with guilt and remorse or do you think they are punishing themselves unnecessarily?

Gabrielle Barnby

GabrielleBarnby works in a variety of genres including poetry and children's fiction. In 2014 her short story *Hostel* appeared in Northwords Now and a selection of her poetry from the St Magnus Festival was published by the George Mackay Brown Fellowship in *Waiting for The Tide*.

Various pieces of her poetry and prose are included in, *Come Sit at Our Table*, a collection of work by the Stromness Writing Group. She is also a contributor to *Kirkwall Visions, Kirkwall Voices*, a creative response to the city supported by the Blide Trust.

Gabrielle's early career was in science. She gained a D.Phil. from Oxford University in 2003 based on research into the molecular basis of autism and has numerous scientific publications on this topic. She began writing fiction after relocating to New Zealand in 2007.

Gabrielle runs workshops for the children's writing group Wirdsmit and is currently editing a collection of their work for publication, she is a also member of the Stromness Writers Group and now lives with her husband and four children in Orkney, Scotland.

Follow Gabrielle:
@GabrielleBarnby
www.gabriellebarnby.com

More Books From ThunderPoint Publishing Ltd.

Mule Train
by Huw Francis
ISBN: 978-0-9575689-0-7 (kindle)
ISBN: 978-0-9575689-1-4 (Paperback)

Four lives come together in the remote and spectacular mountains bordering Afghanistan and explode in a deadly cocktail of treachery, betrayal and violence.

Written with a deep love of Pakistan and the Pakistani people, Mule Train will sweep you from Karachi in the south to the Shandur Pass in the north, through the dangerous borderland alongside Afghanistan, in an adventure that will keep you gripped throughout.

'Stunningly captures the feel of Pakistan, from Karachi to the hills' – tripfiction.com

A Good Death
by Helen Davis
ISBN: 978-0-9575689-7-6 (eBook)
ISBN: 978-0-9575689-6-9 (Paperback)

'A good death is better than a bad conscience,' said Sophie.

1983 – Georgie, Theo, Sophie and Helena, four disparate young Cambridge undergraduates, set out to scale Ausangate, one of the highest and most sacred peaks in the Andes.

Seduced into employing the handsome and enigmatic Wamani as a guide, the four women are initiated into the mystically dangerous side of Peru, Wamani and themselves as they travel from Cuzco to the mountain, a journey that will shape their lives forever.

2013 – though the women are still close, the secrets and betrayals of Ausangate chafe at the friendship.

A girls' weekend at a lonely Fenland farmhouse descends into conflict with the insensitive inclusion of an overbearing young academic toyboy brought along by Theo. Sparked by his unexpected presence, pent up petty jealousies, recriminations and bitterness finally explode the truth of Ausangate, setting the women on a new and dangerous path.

Sharply observant and darkly comic, Helen Davis's début novel is an elegant tale of murder, seduction, vengeance, and the value of a good friendship.

'The prose is crisp, adept, and emotionally evocative' – Lesbrary.com

The Birds That Never Flew
by Margot McCuaig

Shortlisted for the Dundee International Book Prize 2012
Longlisted for the Polari First Book Prize 2014
ISBN: 978-0-9929768-5-9 (eBook)
ISBN: 978-0-9929768-4-2 (Paperback)

'Have you got a light hen? I'm totally gaspin.'

Battered and bruised, Elizabeth has taken her daughter and left her abusive husband Patrick. Again. In the bleak and impersonal Glasgow housing office Elizabeth meets the provocatively intriguing drug addict Sadie, who is desperate to get her own life back on track.

The two women forge a fierce and interdependent relationship as they try to rebuild their shattered lives, but despite their bold, and sometimes illegal attempts it seems impossible to escape from the abuse they have always known, and tragedy strikes.

More than a decade later Elizabeth has started to implement her perfect revenge – until a surreal Glaswegian Virgin Mary steps in with imperfect timing and a less than divine attitude to stick a spoke in the wheel of retribution.

Tragic, darkly funny and irreverent, *The Birds That Never Flew* ushers in a new and vibrant voice in Scottish literature.

'...dark, beautiful and moving, I wholeheartedly recommend' – scanoir.co.uk

Toxic
by Jackie McLean
Shortlisted for the Yeovil Book Prize 2011
ISBN: 978-0-9575689-8-3 (eBook)
ISBN: 978-0-9575689-9-0 (Paperback)

The recklessly brilliant DI Donna Davenport, struggling to hide a secret from police colleagues and get over the break-up with her partner, has been suspended from duty for a fiery and inappropriate outburst to the press.

DI Evanton, an old-fashioned, hard-living misogynistic copper has been newly demoted for thumping a suspect, and transferred to Dundee with a final warning ringing in his ears and a reputation that precedes him.

And in the peaceful, rolling Tayside farmland a deadly store of MIC, the toxin that devastated Bhopal, is being illegally stored by a criminal gang smuggling the valuable substance necessary for making cheap pesticides.

An anonymous tip-off starts a desperate search for the MIC that is complicated by the uneasy partnership between Davenport and Evanton and their growing mistrust of each others actions.

Compelling and authentic, Toxic is a tense and fast paced crime thriller.

'...a humdinger of a plot that is as realistic as it is frightening' – crimefictionlover.com

In The Shadow Of The Hill
by Helen Forbes
ISBN: 978-0-9929768-1-1 (eBook)
ISBN: 978-0-9929768-0-4 (Paperback)

An elderly woman is found battered to death in the common stairwell of an Inverness block of flats.

Detective Sergeant Joe Galbraith starts what seems like one more depressing investigation of the untimely death of a poor unfortunate who was in the wrong place, at the wrong time.

As the investigation spreads across Scotland it reaches into a past that Joe has tried to forget, and takes him back to the Hebridean island of Harris, where he spent his childhood.

Among the mountains and the stunning landscape of religiously conservative Harris, in the shadow of Ceapabhal, long buried events and a tragic story are slowly uncovered, and the investigation takes on an altogether more sinister aspect.

In The Shadow Of The Hill skilfully captures the intricacies and malevolence of the underbelly of Highland and Island life, bringing tragedy and vengeance to the magical beauty of the Outer Hebrides.

'…our first real home-grown sample of modern Highland noir' – Roger Hutchison; West Highland Free Press

Over Here
by Jane Taylor
ISBN: 978-0-9929768-3-5 (eBook)
ISBN: 978-0-9929768-2-8 (Paperback)

'It's coming up to twenty-four hours since the boy stepped down from the big passenger liner – it must be, he reckons foggily – because morning has come around once more with the awful irrevocability of time destined to lead nowhere in this worrying new situation. His temporary minder on board – last spotted heading for the bar some while before the lumbering process of docking got underway – seems to have vanished for good. Where does that leave him now? All on his own in a new country: that's where it leaves him. He is just nine years old.'

An eloquently written novel tracing the social transformations of a century where possibilities were opened up by two world wars that saw millions of men move around the world to fight, and mass migration to the new worlds of Canada and Australia by tens of thousands of people looking for a better life.

Through the eyes of three generations of women, the tragic story of the nine year old boy on Liverpool docks is brought to life in saddeningly evocative prose.

'…a sweeping haunting first novel that spans four generations and two continents…' – Cristina Odone/Catholic Herald

Talk of the Toun
by Helen MacKinven
ISBN: 978-1-910946-00-8 (eBook)
ISBN: 978-0-9929768-7-3 (Paperback)

'She was greetin' again. But there's no need for Lorraine to be feart, since the first day of primary school, Angela has always been there to mop up her tears and snotters.'

An uplifting black comedy of love, family life and friendship, Talk of the Toun is a bittersweet coming-of-age tale set in the summer of 1985, in working class, central belt Scotland.

Lifelong friends Angela and Lorraine are two very different girls, with a growing divide in their aspirations and ambitions putting their friendship under increasing strain.

Artistically gifted Angela has her sights set on art school, but lassies like Angela, from a small town council scheme, are expected to settle for a nice wee secretarial job at the local factory. Her only ally is her gallus gran, Senga, the pet psychic, who firmly believes that her granddaughter can be whatever she wants.

Though Lorraine's ambitions are focused closer to home Angela has plans for her too, and a caravan holiday to Filey with Angela's family tests the dynamics of their relationship and has lifelong consequences for them both.

Effortlessly capturing the religious and social intricacies of 1980s Scotland, Talk of the Toun is the perfect mix of pathos and humour as the two girls wrestle with the complications of growing up and exploring who they really are.

'Fresh, fierce and funny...a sharp and poignant study of growing up in 1980s Scotland. You'll laugh, you'll cry...you'll cringe' – KAREN CAMPBELL

Lightning Source UK Ltd.
Milton Keynes UK
UKOW06f0924051015

259863UK00006B/34/P